Without wa
sweater ove

"I never would h...............................girl," he murmured with a faint note of amusement as he eyed her utilitarian bra.

"Cotton's comfortable," she protested breathlessly.

"It's also not the least bit erotic." Imprisoning both her wrists in one hand, he released the front catch with a deft flick of his wrist.

"I would think I should be allowed to wear whatever I please," she whispered as her heart started to beat faster. Harder. "The days are my own."

"I lied." The long hard fingers of his right hand cupped her breast. "Feel how your body warms to my touch," he said. He lifted her breast and kissed the pale crevice beneath it, causing heat to pool in her lower body.

"I could take you right now. I could make you come…again and again. I could give you the best sex of your life, Gillian. And leave you begging for more…"

His words both shocked and aroused her. And somehow bound her to him as inexorably as a pair of velvet handcuffs might bind her to his bed.

Blaze™

Dear Reader,

Harlequin Blaze is a supersexy new series. If you like love stories with a strong sexual edge, then this is the line for you! The books are fun and flirtatious, the heroes are hot and outrageous. Blaze is a series for the woman who wants *more* in her reading pleasure....

This month, *USA Today* bestselling author JoAnn Ross brings you #5 *Thirty Nights,* a provocative story about a man who wants a woman for only thirty nights of sheer pleasure. Then popular Kimberly Raye poses the question of what women really expect in a man, in the sizzling #6 *The Pleasure Principle.* Talented Candace Schuler delivers #7 *Uninhibited,* a hot story with two fiery protagonists who have few inhibitions—about each other! Carly Phillips rounds out the month with another SEXY CITY NIGHTS story set in New York—where the heat definitely escalates after dark...

Look for four Blaze books every month at your favorite bookstore. And check us out online at eHarlequin.com and tryblaze.com.

Enjoy!

Birgit Davis-Todd
Senior Editor & Editorial Coordinator
Harlequin Blaze

THIRTY NIGHTS

JoAnn Ross

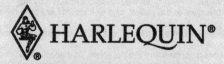

HARLEQUIN®

TORONTO • NEW YORK • LONDON
AMSTERDAM • PARIS • SYDNEY • HAMBURG
STOCKHOLM • ATHENS • TOKYO • MILAN • MADRID
PRAGUE • WARSAW • BUDAPEST • AUCKLAND

ISBN 0-373-79009-0

THIRTY NIGHTS

This edition published by arrangement with Harlequin Books S.A.

® and TM are trademarks of the publisher. Trademarks indicated with
® are registered in the United States Patent and Trademark Office, the
Canadian Trade Marks Office and in other countries.

Visit us at www.eHarlequin.com

Printed in U.S.A.

A NOTE FROM THE AUTHOR...

I'd like to share a secret with you: *Thirty Nights* was not originally written for publication. It began as a story I made up to amuse myself——and my husband——while snowed in at our mountain cabin. My personal fantasies have always revolved around the dark and dangerous. Even as a child I preferred Beauty's Beast to Cinderella's Prince, Batman to Superman, and my favorite movie was *The Phantom of the Opera*.

I adore reluctant heroes with tragic pasts, men who've put themselves in harm's way and have been wounded, physically, emotionally, or both in the process. Hunter St. John is such a man: the quintessential "beast" hiding away on his remote island, he's built an impenetrable wall around his emotions. But Gillian Cassidy is determined to tear down that hateful wall, unlock those chains around his heart and expose Hunter to the healing powers of love.

Thirty Nights is a very special book to me. Writing it allowed me to follow my characters on their edgy, erotic journey. Hunter is not an easy man to love, but by the time I wrote The End, Gillian and I had both fallen madly, passionately in love with him. I hope you will, too.

I love to hear from readers. You can write to me or sign up for an electronic newsletter at www.joannross.com.

Warmest,

JoAnn Ross

Prologue

TO A CASUAL VISITOR, the leafy campus of the Massachusetts Institute of Technology, located on the banks of the Charles River, would appear to be a peaceful glade. In this case, appearances were definitely deceiving. Inside a sixty-year-old ivy covered red brick building a battle royal was raging.

Hunter St. John was furious enough to kill the man he'd mistakenly considered a mentor. If this had been the Stone Age, he would have picked up the nearest club and bashed George Cassidy's head in. Civilization being what it was, he was forced to fight with mere words.

"You stole my research and used it as your own."

"There you go again, being overly dramatic." The older man dismissed the complaint with a brief wave of his hand. "Sometimes I worry about you, St. John."

"The gene-splicing project was mine," Hunter insisted.

"You're my research assistant, everything you do while a student here rightfully belongs to me. Including that little gene-splicing experiment."

"That little gene-splicing experiment just won you

a research grant from the National Institutes of Health, dammit.''

Cassidy's features took on an expression of smug satisfaction. "It was well deserved."

"It was my project." Hunter's growl was that of a wolf who'd just come across an interloper approaching his den. "I came up with it, I pushed it, I babied it along, going without sleep to work on it during hours I wasn't working on your research. You had no right to it."

To Hunter's amazement, Cassidy actually had the nerve to smile. "You're a bright young man, St. John. However, I fear that you lack the emotional restraint necessary to succeed in the research field. Along with a keen intellect and a deep-seated curiosity, a scientist must possess a clear and cool head. Which you lack. Which is why I regrettably had to notify the administration you were no longer suited to work here."

Hunter had always known George Cassidy to be an egotistical, coldhearted son of a bitch. Since that seemed to be the norm in the world of scientific research, he hadn't been particularly bothered by his behavior. But this treachery was beyond anything even he could have imagined.

"You had me taken off the project? I'm canned?"

"That's not exactly the word I would have chosen, but yes."

A fury like nothing he'd ever before experienced surged through Hunter. He curled his hands into fists at his sides to keep from pounding them into the supercilious bastard's handsome face. "I could kill you."

"Oh, you wouldn't want to do that," Cassidy countered. "Believe me, Hunter, my boy, the laboratory facilities in prison are definitely not up to your standards.''

When Hunter didn't even bother to respond, the older man shook his head in mock remorse. ''You're making too much of this,'' he repeated. ''You're a young man, only twenty years old—''

''I'm twenty-one.'' Following in his brilliant late father's footsteps, he'd already garnered a medical degree from Harvard and a master's in biochemistry from MIT. The gene-splicing project Cassidy had so blithely pirated had been Hunter's doctoral work.

''You're still a wet-behind-the-ears pup. There will be more projects for you to work on.''

''I had a project, dammit. Until it was stolen from me.''

''Really, my boy, your choice of words is not only inaccurate, it's redundant.'' Appearing bored with this conversation, Cassidy opened a cage, pulled out a white research rabbit and prepared to draw a blood sample.

It was not in Hunter's nature to surrender without a fight. ''I could go to the administration and tell them what you've done.''

''And whom do you think they'd believe? A student who's already been thrown out of two undergraduate schools due to his hot temper? Or a respected, world-renowned, award-winning scientist who's on the shortlist to be nominated for the Nobel Prize?''

Both men knew the answer to that rhetorical question. Just as they both knew that Hunter's time here had come to an abrupt, inglorious end.

''If you ever manage to control your unruly emotions,'' Cassidy said into the silence that had settled over the laboratory, "you could well prove to be one of the greatest scientific minds of our time. But there's one thing you need to learn."

Hunter felt as if he were suffocating. "What's that?"

The older man absently stroked the rabbit's soft white fur. "It's a bunny-eat-bunny world out there. Survival goes to the fittest."

And the most treacherous, Hunter thought. And although he knew that it would only confirm Cassidy's belief that he was too emotional to be a ground-breaking scientist, what was proving more irritating to Hunter than the theft of his research project was the realization that such betrayal had come from a man he trusted. A man he'd foolishly come to think of as a surrogate father.

"I'll make you pay for this."

"Perhaps." Cassidy remained seemingly unperturbed by the gritty threat. "In the meantime, please shut the door on your way out. I wouldn't want the rabbits to get ill from a draft."

A crimson curtain, born of his boiling fury, drifted over Hunter's eyes. Wanting to escape before he beat his former mentor to a bloody pulp with his bare fists, he stormed from the laboratory. Blinded by rage as he was, he didn't even notice that he'd almost run into Cassidy's young daughter.

Clad in the Catholic school uniform of a prim white blouse and green plaid skirt, Gillian Cassidy clutched her schoolbooks to her still-flat chest and watched Hunter St. John stride down the hall.

He was leaving. He and her father had fought before. Yet she knew, with every fiber of her young being, that this time Hunter would not be back.

Biting her bottom lip to block the involuntary whimper that rose in her throat, she closed her eyes, leaned back against the muddy-green wall and considered miserably that although her famed father supposedly knew everything there was to know about the human body, she suddenly possessed a unique medical knowledge of her own.

Although she was only twelve years old, Gillian now knew exactly how excruciatingly painful it was for a human heart to break.

1

RIO HAD AN INFECTIOUS BEAT and a beauty all its own. The pace was fast, the Cariocas' celebrated zest for living readily evident, particularly after midnight when stunningly attractive people crowded the pink tile sidewalks and packed the clubs.

Gillian Cassidy's dressing room boasted a breathtaking view of Guanabara Bay, but her attention was not on the dancing lights surrounding the worldfamous gumdrop-shaped peak of Sugarloaf Mountain. Instead, she was conducting a postmortem of the midnight show she'd just completed with her road manager. It was her first piano concert in the Brazilian city; she had four more performances over the next two nights before moving on to Australia.

The room was filled to overflowing with flowers. One elaborate arrangement of gladiolus and calla lilies was from the theater management. A dazzling display of lacy orange bird-of-paradise blooms and giant scarlet poppies was a gift from the American ambassador, who'd flown in from La Paz. The rest were from fans and admirers from all over the country.

"What did you think of the lighting?" she asked

as she sat down at the dressing table. She'd changed from the long black evening gown into a white terry-cloth robe.

"I thought it was perfect. As always," Deke Feller assured her. He opened the minibar and took out a bottle of Brazilian beer for himself and mineral water for Gillian.

"You didn't think the blue light during the 'Dreams' number was a little too cool?" She dipped her finger into a small porcelain pot and began to smooth the fragrant cold cream over her face.

"I told you, I thought it was perfect."

"I still think it could have been warmer." The perfume from the blooms was overwhelming; she was beginning to get a headache. Gillian made a mental note to send the bouquets to local hospitals. "What would you say to adding a touch of pink?"

"Pink," he repeated on a deliberately bland tone as he jotted the change down in the notebook he was never without.

She looked at him in the mirror. "You don't agree?"

"I told you," he said with a shrug, his accent revealing Tennessee roots that predated the Confederacy, "I thought it looked great. But you're the star."

And if the star wanted pink, then the lighting crew would damn well oblige, Gillian knew. She'd heard rumors that the macho Brazilian crew, unaccustomed to such unrelenting attention to detail from a mere female, was accusing her of being a bitch. Dealing with critics had taught her to shrug off negative remarks. Even so, the accusation stung.

Gillian frowned. "Do you think I'm a prima donna?"

She'd been working with Deke for three years. During that time he'd become the closest thing Gillian had to a best friend, and unlike so many other of her employees, who tended to tell her what she wanted to hear, she could trust him to be honest with her. Even when it hurt.

"Of course not." Deke appeared surprised by that idea. "You may be a perfectionist, Gilly. But that's what makes you sell out all your performances everywhere we go."

Gillian had realized in her first days of the music business, when she'd been just another struggling pianist trying to carve out a niche in a field dominated by country and pop artists, that the business was every bit as important as the music.

The challenge, of course, was to try to balance the magic and bliss of the music with insisting on using her own microphones for the auditorium PA systems and having her accountant keep a close eye on her record company royalty statements.

She also understood that too often people made the mistake of thinking that just because she looked soft, she did business that way, too. Over the years she'd acquired an agent, manager, producer and more people than she could easily count working with her and for her. Still, she insisted on making the final decision on even seemingly unimportant details, from what color lipstick she'd wear on stage to the typeface used for the programs.

Was it so wrong to want fans to feel as if they'd gotten their money's worth? she wondered, even as she reluctantly admitted that her almost obsessive need to govern all aspects of her life had been born that long-ago day when her father had phoned her at her Swiss boarding school to unemotionally inform her that he was divorcing her slut of a mother.

"Besides," Deke drawled, his deep voice breaking into her introspection, "my Aunt Fayrene had a saying."

"Was she the one who sang in the Grand Ole Opry?"

Shaking off her uncharacteristic gloomy self-doubts, Gillian wiped the cold cream and heavy stage makeup off with a tissue. She'd given up trying to keep Deke's countless relatives straight.

"Uh-uh." He shook his head, took a long swallow of beer, sighed his pleasure, then wiped the foam off his mouth with the back of his hand. "That was Aunt Patsy. Aunt Fayrene's the one who ran the Rebel's Roost outside Turkey Gulch."

"Of course," Gillian murmured. "However could I forget the infamous madam of Turkey Gulch, Tennessee's most popular house of ill repute?"

"Laugh all you want, but Fayrene was one smart cookie. She realized that since so many women were more than willing to give sex away, she had to think of herself as bein' in the entertainment business."

"Now you're comparing me to a prostitute?" Amused, Gillian sipped her mineral water and felt her exhaustion begin to slip away.

"Hell, no. But what Aunt Fayrene always said about the hooker who realized she was sitting on the gold mine fits your situation." He flashed her the grin that she suspected had charmed a great many Southern belles.

"You've got a lot of pretty glittery gold to sell, Gilly. The trick is not to let anyone go prospectin' without first paying for the mineral rights."

Gillian laughed as she was meant to. "I'll keep that in mind."

Castle Mountain, Maine

HUNTER ST. JOHN LAY in bed, enjoying the aftermath of passion. The woman snuggled up against him was a biochemist working at the nearby think tank colloquially referred to by the locals as the "brain factory." Toni Maggione was intelligent, driven, seductive, and what was most appealing to Hunter, she possessed an unrelentingly hedonistic attitude toward sex.

They'd first met three years ago, when, following his release from a Bosnian hospital, he'd arrived on the remote island off the rocky coast of Maine to work on his latest project. After a brief verbal exchange of personal résumés, and even briefer explanations of their works in progress, she'd leaned against a stainless steel table in her laboratory and chewed on a short scarlet fingernail while studying him, as if he were one of the lab animals she was considering using for her cancer research. He'd watched her gaze flick over his scarred and disfigured face, waiting for the expected response of horror, but all he'd read in those coffee-dark eyes had been vague curiosity.

"Three of my rats died this morning," she'd told him.

"Should I say I'm sorry?"

"That's not necessary. Since it wouldn't change the fact that they died. And I was so hoping for a remission." Her full lips had pouted. "It's been a horrid morning."

"Perhaps it'll get better."

Her smile had been slow and openly provocative. "You must be a mind reader. Because that's precisely what I was thinking." Her hips had swayed enticingly as she'd crossed the white tile laboratory floor in a way that had reminded him of a lioness on the hunt and locked the door. Then, still smiling, she'd turned back toward him and had begun taking off her clothes. Not waiting for a verbal invitation, Hunter had quickly shed his, as well.

They'd continued to get together three or four times a month. Constantly underfunded, suffering frustrating setbacks that were part and parcel of medical research, Dr. Antoinette Maggione used sex to relieve the unrelenting pressure of her work. Possessing a strong sex drive himself, Hunter was more than willing to help her out.

"I almost forgot. I brought you a present," she said, slipping from his arms.

"A present?"

She laughed at the unmistakable alarm in his voice. "Don't panic, darling." Reaching up, she patted his scarred cheek. "You've already insisted that I'm not allowed to get you a Christmas present again this year," she reminded him. "This is just a little something I saw in the video store the other day." She left the bed, went into the living room and returned with the boxed tape. "I thought at the time that it might add to the mood."

Hunter pushed himself up into a sitting position. "If you need a porno tape to get in the mood, I must not being doing my job."

She laughed again. "Darling, if you weren't a magnificent lover, I wouldn't have forgotten about the

tape two minutes after you opened the door. It isn't
pornography. It's a music video.''

She turned on the bedroom television and stuck the
tape into the VCR, then slipped back into bed.

Piano music filled the room. Hunter had never considered himself even a remotely fanciful man, yet the
way it flowed, clean and clear, vaguely reminded him
of a sunlit river tumbling over mossy rocks on the
way to the sea.

On the screen, a slender woman was seated in a
circle of towering stones. Her back was to the camera,
her long hair—a blend of red, copper and gold that
brought to mind a dazzling sunset—fell in rippling
waves to her waist.

"I wonder how the producer got permission to film
at Stonehenge,'' he wondered out loud.

Toni shrugged her bare shoulders. "Gillian Cassidy's sales figures probably speak pretty loudly. Fac-
tor in her incredible looks and I doubt if there's a
male government bureaucrat anywhere in the world
who'd be able to say no to the woman. There are also
some incredible scenes set on the Irish coast.''

"Cassidy?''

His nemesis's surname rang an instant and unpleasant bell. It was, Hunter reminded himself, a not un-
common name. Especially along the eastern seaboard
where so many immigrants of Irish extraction had settled.

But didn't George Cassidy have a daughter? He
vaguely remembered a skinny little thing with wild
carrot-hued hair that was always escaping her braids,
and a mouthful of metal braces.

"If you'd ever get your head out of the laboratory,
you'd know that Gillian Cassidy just happens to be

the hottest New Age performer in the country,'' Toni informed him. ''Last year her *Machu Picchu* CD outsold John Tesh's and Yanni's albums combined. This one went platinum in the first week.''

As the slender hands flowed over the keyboard, the music grew richer, more complicated, soothing his mind even as it stirred his blood. It couldn't be the same girl, Hunter assured himself. George Cassidy had always seemed more android than man; from what Hunter had witnessed, the scientist hadn't possessed a single iota of human emotion.

The idea that such an unfeeling bastard could have fathered a child capable of tapping into such deep-seated primal passions merely by skimming her fingertips over eighty-eight ebony and ivory keys was inconceivable.

The view shifted as the camera lens went in for a close-up of the pianist's face. Unaware of doing so, Hunter leaned closer toward the screen.

She was looking down at the keys, but as he watched, seemingly in response to his unspoken command, she slowly lifted her gaze.

Pow! Hunter experienced what felt like a body blow as he found himself staring straight into a pair of thickly lashed green eyes that were simultaneously both foreign and familiar. Unbelievably, it was her. Damned if Cassidy's little girl hadn't grown up. Which, Hunter allowed, only made sense, since the planet certainly hadn't stopped spinning since that long-ago day when his mentor had betrayed him.

Her velvety soft eyes, which he recalled having been once hidden by thick, tortoise-shell-framed glasses that had seemed oversize on her small face, tilted up, catlike, at the corners. Her complexion was the pale alabaster of a true redhead, and either she'd neglected to paint her lips or the makeup person for the video shoot had selected a pale pink the color of the inside of a seashell.

When a faint breeze picked up a few strands of hair and blew them across those slightly parted pink lips, hunger stirred, deep and unbidden.

She looked as fragile as blown glass. But the music flowing from those unlacquered fingertips was as potent as Irish whiskey. And every bit as intoxicating.

She appeared to have inherited her mother's passion. Hunter recalled George Cassidy's third wife, Irene, being a great deal younger than her husband and a great deal less restrained.

Yet the one trait both Cassidys had shared had been their unrelenting, unapologetic aggressiveness in going after what they wanted. At the time, Irene Cassidy had certainly wanted him.

"Well, I'd thought the tape might set a sexy mood." Toni's husky voice was a blend of amusement and feminine pique. "But I didn't expect competition."

Music from the stereo speakers swelled around him, in him, like a fever in the blood.

"Don't talk nonsense. You're in a league of your own, sweetheart." He pulled her close and kissed her with more affection than lust.

It was times like this, when his body was sated and his mind pleasantly fogged, free from the burden of romantic entanglements, when Hunter understood that George Cassidy had been right about one thing. Emotions were unnecessary complications. They weakened a man, made him vulnerable.

During the thirteen years since he'd left MIT,

Hunter had survived—indeed prospered—by burying his feelings so deeply inside him he could no longer remember the idealistic young man he'd once been. Hunter supposed he should be grateful to Cassidy for that.

As Toni snuggled against him again, his mind continued to drift to thoughts of Cassidy and his daughter, whose appearance reminded him of one of those ethereal angels painted on the domed ceilings of Renaissance cathedrals.

He wondered idly if she were actually as virginal as she seemed, then remembering the depths of passion that had flowed from those fingertips, decided she couldn't possibly be.

But the contrast of passion and innocence was undeniably appealing. What would it take, he mused, to make that serene, delicate woman scream with wild, wanton pleasure?

Suddenly, Hunter, who had not celebrated any holiday since that fateful afternoon he'd packed his bags and left MIT, knew exactly what he wanted for Christmas.

He wanted Gillian Cassidy. And thanks to what he knew about her formerly celebrated father, he intended to have her.

2

"GOOD GOD, MAN!" The scientist stared at his former protégé. "You can't be serious."

"On the contrary, I've never been more serious in my life," Hunter responded mildly.

The fact that George Cassidy had not been able to resist accepting the summons to Castle Mountain from his former student was proof that the power between them had shifted. It was an acknowledgment, of sorts, Hunter thought with satisfaction, that the student had now become the master.

Oh, Cassidy was still a respected researcher and teacher.

His articles still routinely appeared in scientific journals and he was a frequent speaker at conferences. But it had escaped no one's notice that he hadn't come up with a truly important breakthrough in a decade.

His star was on the decline. While Hunter's, which had taken off like a comet after he'd been forced from MIT, was now fixed as the brightest in the scientific firmament. Hunter couldn't count the number of requests for speeches he turned down in any given month.

And unlike Cassidy, whose lectures were usually

scheduled for the Sunday morning on the last day of a conference, when attendees were more likely to be worried about packing and making planes than listening to a rehash of old data, Hunter was routinely invited to be the keynote speaker at the most prestigious gatherings in the world.

Not that he appeared in person any longer, of course, but his recorded speeches—audio only, never video—were enough to draw standing-room-only crowds.

Hunter had been an intensely private man even before the assassination attempt that had disfigured him, and his reclusive behavior fueled various rumors. Two of the more recurring ones were that he'd become scarred beyond recognition and/or that he'd become the quintessential mad scientist creating Lord knows what sort of genetic mutations in his island laboratory. Hunter didn't really give a damn what people said about him, as long as they left him alone.

The older man shook his head. Although at first glance George Cassidy had the look of a lion in winter, his thick mane of snowy hair had thinned, Hunter noticed irrelevantly. His once patrician nose was red and bulbous, indicating that his fondness for alcohol had intensified.

"This has to be some sort of sick joke."

"I never joke." Hunter leaned back in his leather chair, braced his elbows on the arms and eyed Cassidy over the tent of his fingers. "As you once so succinctly told me, emotions get in the way of logic. Which means, I suppose," he allowed, "I owe a great deal of my success to your advice."

"You would have succeeded on your own."

"True. But if you hadn't gotten me taken off the project, you would have continued to take credit for my work." Work that had taken off in an entirely new direction, partly due to this man's treachery. If Cassidy hadn't stolen his research, he might never have developed such an interest in the age-old nature versus nurture argument.

"That's what this is all about, isn't it? You told me someday I'd pay. And now you're out for revenge."

"*Revenge* is such an unpleasant word, don't you think?" Hunter countered pleasantly. "And actually, you're wrong, Cassidy. I gave up on that idea a very long time ago. After I realized that you were no longer a very formidable adversary."

He flashed a smile Toni had once described as being as merciless as a rattler's. "Victory against a paper tiger isn't much of a victory."

The words obviously struck home, causing the older man to flinch. Better watch those emotions, George, Hunter thought. Or they'll be your downfall yet.

"Then why—"

"It's simple. As I said, your daughter has matured into a talented, lovely woman. And I want her."

"You make her sound like a possession, like a car. Gillian isn't some inanimate bauble to be bought and sold. She's a woman—"

"I'm well aware of that. It's precisely why I want her," Hunter interjected patiently.

"My point is, she isn't mine to give. The girl hasn't

lived under my roof since her mother and I divorced when she was barely in her teens.''

''But you kept in touch.''

Remembering those intimate little faculty dinners where Irene Cassidy had inevitably managed to corner him in some private corner of the professor's Cape Cod house and attempt, unsuccessfully, to seduce him, Hunter suspected the woman wasn't the type who'd willingly go to work to support herself and a young daughter.

''To some extent.'' Cassidy's next words confirmed Hunter's thoughts. ''Although my attorney fought her every step of the way, Irene managed to get the judge to award her a hefty alimony settlement. She also demanded—and won—hefty boarding school and college tuition payments. Naturally, I demanded equally generous holiday visitation rights.''

''Naturally,'' Hunter said dryly.

He had the impression that neither parent had cared all that much for the teenage girl whose life must have been turned upside down by an acrimonious divorce. Gillian Cassidy had been merely a useful pawn in a war between two self-absorbed egoists.

Not so different from his own upbringing, he considered. However, in his case, neither of his illustrious, selfish parents could be bothered with the son they'd created more to ensure their immortality than out of any sense of lasting love. For each other or their child.

''But even if Gilly didn't have a mind of her own, which believe me, despite that cotton-candy exterior, she does have,'' Cassidy continued, ''the days of fathers marrying off their daughters—''

''Who said anything about marriage?'' Hunter cut him off again. ''Marriage is for fools who believe in love and all its accompanying complications. Your own experience in the marital sweepstakes should have taught you that it doesn't work.

''I want Gillian for one thing. And one thing only. For sex.''

''That's obscene!''

Hunter lifted a brow. ''Since when were you elected arbiter of society's morals, Cassidy?''

Gillian's father didn't answer. Instead, he continued to stare at Hunter, as if he were some sort of monster. Which, Hunter allowed, he just might be.

''What the hell happened to you?'' Cassidy asked quietly. Carefully.

Hunter's ironic smile was grim and twisted and revealed not an iota of humor. ''As you once warned me, it's bunny-eat-bunny out there. And even in our business, research can get a little risky.''

The memory of the letter bomb exploding in his hand flashed like lightning in his mind. A memory of burning flesh seared his nostrils; inhuman screams, torn from his own throat, reverberated in his head. Utilizing the steely control that had kept him alive during those long and painful months of recuperation and rehabilitation, Hunter closed the door on the unbidden flashback.

''Now, since the forecast calls for an evening storm and I don't believe either of us cares to be stuck here in close proximity while we wait for it to blow over,

I'm going to cut right to the chase and save us both time so you can return to Cambridge....

"The fact is that I fancy your daughter. I've been thinking about her too much lately, and those thoughts are disturbing my work. So, I've come to the conclusion that the logical thing to do is to get the woman out of my system.

"I could take the time to go through some lengthy, ridiculous courtship routine, and, since I've been assured that despite certain obvious physical disadvantages, I'm a fairly good catch, I have no doubt that I could seduce her without a great deal of difficulty.

"However, since I possess neither the time nor the patience for such social game playing, I've decided to put the problem into your hands."

"My hands?"

"It's quite simple. I expect you to convince your daughter to come here to Maine, where I assure you, she will be treated with consideration and respect. I will not physically harm her. Nor will I play with her emotions the way so many lovers might.

"I've read that she's just coming off a grueling tour and needs a rest. I'm offering leisurely days spent in a remote, idyllic location.

"As for her nights—" he enjoyed watching the older man flinch as he flashed a wicked, sexually suggestive grin "—I won't bore you with the details."

"You're a devil, St. John." Cassidy's nervous eyes drifted to the twisted red-and-white flesh that ran from temple to jaw on the left side of Hunter's face.

"Perhaps. I'm also a man, Cassidy." Hunter's tone remained as detached as his unblinking gaze. "A man with needs. Which is where the lovely Gillian comes in. And when those needs have been sufficiently satisfied, I'll send her back to you. Safe and sound.''

"What makes you think I'd lift a finger to help you sleep with my daughter?''

Cassidy was shaking with rage; his face was so red Hunter wondered idly if he were on the verge of having a stroke. He also wondered if somehow he'd stumbled upon the old man's soft spot. Perhaps he did care for his only daughter, after all.

"The stories I've heard about your diminishing capacity must be true.'' Hunter shook his head with mock regret. "You are losing it, George, old man. The reason you'll convince your daughter to join me here is because if you don't, I'll go public with what happened thirteen years ago.''

The older man blanched, the color fading from his too bright cheeks. "You couldn't prove a thing!''

"That's where you're wrong. But it's a moot point. Because the tables have turned. Whom do you think people would believe? A man recently voted the most brilliant scientist of his time? Or a broken-down has-been, clinging desperately to tenure with both hands, while trying to drown his failures in a bottle?''

"You wouldn't.''

Hunter looked him straight in the eye. "In a heartbeat.''

He stood up and looked dispassionately down at Cassidy. "Since I have no desire to interrupt her tour, I'll give Gillian seven days to show up.''

"If it were up to me, I'd send her to you,'' George said. "But she's always been ridiculously stubborn.

Even those ruler-wielding Swiss nuns at the convent school in Lucerne couldn't make the girl do anything she didn't want to."

He shook his leonine head again and looked balefully up at Hunter. "I'll try. But I can't promise anything."

His former mentor's response proved that there were no depths to which he'd sink to save his miserable career and overblown reputation. Despite his victory, Hunter found himself vaguely sickened by Cassidy's willingness to act as pimp for his own daughter.

"Now, that's where we're different again. Because I can promise something. I promise to ruin you if Gillian isn't here by the end of the week."

With a defeated slump of his shoulders—though for himself or for his daughter, Hunter wasn't quite sure—Cassidy silently left the room.

As Hunter stood at the window, watching the car that was taking Cassidy back down the cliff, he allowed himself, just this once, to enjoy the feeling of long-overdue satisfaction.

Then, as he remembered Gillian Cassidy's soft green eyes and lush pale mouth, satisfaction gave way to anticipation.

Cambridge

GILLIAN COULDN'T BELIEVE what she was hearing.

"Let me get this straight." She dragged her hand through her hair and faced her father across the lush Persian carpet covering the mahogany-plank study floor. "After thirteen years, Hunter St. John suddenly invites you to his home, then threatens to blackmail you?"

"The man's a devil," Cassidy grumbled, pouring another two fingers of whiskey into the Waterford old-fashioned glass.

"So you've said."

Gillian was having trouble with that idea. Although she admittedly may have once gazed at Hunter St. John through foolishly romantic, rose-colored glasses, she didn't believe her father's harshly derogatory description fit.

There was something more to all this. Something her father wasn't telling her.

"But it doesn't make any sense," she argued, every instinct she possessed on alert. She couldn't remember once, in all her twenty-five years, her father ever revealing this much emotion. "You're a respected scientist. How could Hunter possibly ruin your reputation?"

A log shifted on the fire, creating a shower of sparks. Appearing openly grateful for the diversion, George leaped from his bark brown leather chair and began jabbing at the fragrant applewood with the poker.

Gillian was not to be distracted. "I asked you a question, Father. Does Hunter know something you've neglected to mention? Was there something about the project you two were working on—"

"We weren't working on any project together!" George's ruddy cheeks were made even brighter by his anger. "Hunter St. John was a graduate lab assis-

tant. No different from hundreds of others who have
worked for me over the years.''

''He was obviously more intelligent than most,''
she pointed out. ''While flying back from New Zealand, I read in *Newsweek* that many in the scientific
community consider him a genius.''

Wondering how old a woman had to get before she
outgrew schoolgirl crushes, Gillian had been disgusted by whatever knee-jerk impulse had made her
read the entire cover article. Twice.

The bombing that had nearly killed him had made
the news, and although details had been sketchy, reports at the time had suggested that the assassination
attempt was due to some top secret government project he'd been working on. The *Newsweek* journalist
had reported that while Hunter had recovered well
enough to resume his work—which had relieved Gillian greatly—he'd subsequently become more reclusive than ever. The fact that he'd refused to be inter-
viewed for the article had not surprised Gillian, who
remembered Hunter being very private.

''The man's bright enough,'' Cassidy allowed, his
grudging tone jerking her wandering mind back into
the murky conversational waters. ''In that respect, he
obviously inherited his parents' genes. But Isabel
Montgomery and David St. John were logical, scientific thinkers. Neither could have ever been described as given to emotional tantrums as St. John
unfortunately is. Even during his student days, the
boy was far too headstrong for his own good....

''He refused to follow my instructions, always
thinking he knew best. And he wasn't dependable.''

The still-firm jaw jutted out defiantly. "Which is why I had no choice but to let him go."

"So you said at the time."

That afternoon, like everything else about Hunter, was emblazoned on Gillian's memory. Even now, thirteen years later, she could recall with vivid clarity how livid he'd been when he'd stormed out of the laboratory.

"So." She sat down with a flurry of flowered gauze skirt that was too thin for the frosty December Massachusetts morning, but had been just right when she'd boarded the plane in Auckland fifteen hours earlier. "Since there's no basis for his threat, why are you so concerned?"

"Because he can make waves." George tossed back the whiskey, then refilled the glass, this time nearly to the rim. "St. John always was a loose cannon. A damn troublemaker. If he costs me my tenure—"

"That's ridiculous." While her music was emotional, Gillian had always prided herself on being a woman of unwavering logic. "You achieved tenure years ago, before I was born. The only conceivable way you could possibly lose it would be to..."

Her voice trailed off as a flicker of comprehension began to tease at the back of her mind.

No, she assured herself. It couldn't be true. Nothing had ever been as important to her father as his work. Not his colleagues, his students, his wives, nor his daughter. Gillian had long ago given up trying to win a love he was incapable of giving. But she'd always considered him to be a man of honor.

Unfortunately, as she watched him gulping down the Irish whiskey like a drowning man going under for the third time, she had to wonder.

It made sense, she considered grimly. She'd never believed her father's unpersuasive explanations regarding Hunter leaving the project. And, even more surprisingly, MIT. Students were taken off research projects all the time, for all sorts of reasons. She'd witnessed varying levels of disappointment and frustration. Yet never had she seen the murderous depth of rage she'd witnessed in Hunter that day.

"Father." She leaned forward and put her hand on his knee. "Look at me."

When he reluctantly dragged his gaze to hers, Gillian saw something that looked horrendously like guilt flash across his red-veined eyes.

"Hunter was working toward his doctorate that year," she said slowly. Carefully. "He had his own project—"

"It was a radical, unproved idea."

"Knowing Hunter, that could well be. You always said that he thought outside the box. But if he's as intelligent as everyone says he is—"

"He was on the wrong track," George said, cutting her off with an impatient wave of an unsteady hand. "It wouldn't have worked. It didn't work, until…" This time he was the one to stop in midsentence.

Gillian closed her eyes and rubbed at her temple as the truth struck home.

Dear heavens, she didn't need this. She'd just come off a grueling nine-month tour; she'd caught a cold in London that had stayed with her for weeks; she'd been traveling for hours; and exhaustion was beginning to catch up with her, along with the jet lag she'd been struggling to outrun as she'd raced around the world performing to standing-room-only crowds, talking to the press, trying to remember what she'd said one day in Sydney so as not to repeat herself exactly in Melbourne....

"You stole his project." Her flat tone revealed a deep disappointment she felt all the way to the bone.

"He can't prove a thing," George insisted, dodging the question.

Gillian sighed and allowed herself a moment of profound sadness as her last illusion regarding her father shattered. Then, with a strength of spirit that had gotten her through far worse than this, she began to think the problem through.

"Given Hunter's fame and reputation these days, he wouldn't need to prove his accusation," she mused out loud. "It would be his word against yours. And I'm afraid that just may be a battle you couldn't win." It had, after all, been a very long time since her father had been featured in *Newsweek.*

"That's what I was trying to tell you, dammit," he said grumpily. "The devil's going to cost me everything I've spent my life working for, Gilly."

The headache that had been threatening hit with jackhammer force, pounding at her temple, behind her eyes. As she looked out at the sleet that was being driven against the window, Gillian desperately wished she was back in New Zealand. Or Rio. Anywhere but here.

"I wonder why he waited all these years?"

"That's simple." The alcohol had him slurring his words. "I didn't have anything the black-hearted devil wanted until now."

"I see," Gillian said, not really seeing anything at all. Bone weary, she'd intended to fly straight from Kennedy airport to her beach house in Monterey, where she could spend a restful few weeks recovering from both her cold and the rigors of her tour by sitting out on her deck, watching the whales migrate. She'd been sitting in the first-class lounge, drinking a cup of honey-laced tea that she'd hoped would clear her sinuses but hadn't, waiting to board the flight home, when her father had tracked her down, claiming a life-or-death emergency.

He'd stubbornly refused to be more specific, but concerned enough by the uncharacteristic tremor in his voice, Gillian had immediately changed her plans, taking the plane to Boston instead. Only to discover that the problem wasn't honestly life-threatening at all, merely career-threatening.

Then again, Gillian reminded herself wearily, her father's work had always been his life.

"What does Hunter want, Father?"

He stared at her through blurry, glazed eyes. "Didn't I tell you?"

"No."

"He wants you, Gilly. The heartless, amoral bastard says that if I don't send you to Maine to sleep with him for thirty nights, he'll ruin me. He gave me seven days to get you there. That was three days ago. I've only got four days left before I'm ruined."

He shook his head. Then, muttering something about devils and the lowest circles of hell, George Cassidy passed out.

3

Castle Mountain

TWENTY-FOUR HOURS PAST the deadline, Gillian still hadn't shown up on the island. Frustrated and disgusted with himself for the way he'd been watching the clock, Hunter had driven to the think tank located a few miles from his house, where he'd tried, with scant success, to concentrate on work.

"I figured you'd be working at home today," a familiar voice said.

Hunter glanced back over his shoulder and saw Dylan Prescott standing in the doorway. Dylan, the founder of the think tank, was extraordinarily brilliant and unrelentingly good-natured. His sister was police chief and he was married to a science fiction writer whose stunningly cool beauty defied every nerdy stereotype regarding the mostly male genre.

More important, Dylan was also one of the few individuals Hunter trusted without hesitation. They weren't working in the same fields—Dylan's area of interest and expertise was space and time travel—yet Hunter enjoyed running hypotheses by his friend. Invariably, the imaginative scientist would come up with a new twist that Hunter hadn't considered.

"Why would you think that?"

Dylan shrugged. "I dropped into the Gray Gull for coffee this morning before coming here. Ben Adams mentioned something about having to pick up a guest of yours from the mainland on his mail packet."

He was too polite to ask, and too good a friend to probe into personal matters, but Hunter knew Dylan was curious. Especially since Hunter wasn't known to entertain all that many guests at his remote, well-guarded home.

It was his turn to shrug. "That's up in the air," he said vaguely.

Dylan gave him a probing look, then, knowing his friend well, apparently decided that there was no point in digging. "It's just as well you're here," he said. "Since you've got a visitor."

"Oh?" He wondered if Ben had actually brought Gillian here, instead of to the house as he'd instructed.

"It's that *GQ* guy from State," Dylan revealed. "He's currently cooling his heels in the reception area."

Hunter shook his head. A government bureaucrat was just what he needed to top off a less-than-perfect day. He cursed. Then, remembering that the government was paying the bills for his research, sighed with resignation.

"I suppose, since he's come all this way, I'm going to have to see him."

"I'll go tell Janet to send him in, then," Dylan said.

As the receptionist ushered the man into his outer office, it crossed Hunter's mind that if Hollywood ever went looking for someone to cast in the role of a rising player in the high-stakes world of international diplomacy, James Van Horn would be perfect for the part. His hundred-dollar haircut and cashmere coat suggested the family wealth Hunter knew had made him a legendary undergrad at Princeton. The British accent he tended to affect was a reminder of his days at Oxford, and his shoes—wing tips, for God's sake—were far more appropriate for walking the marbled halls of the State Department than wading through Castle Mountain's snowdrifts.

"I wasn't expecting you." Annoyed by the intrusion, and even more irritated that the man wasn't the woman he'd been expecting for the past twenty-four hours, Hunter didn't bother with pleasantries.

"I suppose you wouldn't believe that I was in the neighborhood and decided to drop in and see how the work was progressing."

"Not on a bet."

Without waiting for an invitation, he took off his coat, which he hung with precision on the coatrack, hitched up the legs of his wool suit slacks, sat down in a leather chair, crossed his legs, then ran his manicured fingers down a knife-sharp crease.

"I had business in New England." Shoulders clad in a subdued gray pinstripe shrugged. "You weren't that far out of my way."

It was a lie and both men knew it. Hunter waited him out.

"So, are the rumors true?" Van Horn eventually asked.

"Which rumors are you referring to?"

"The ones circulating around Washington that you're on the verge of finalizing the project."

The project in question was an offshoot of the gene studies Hunter had been doing when George Cassidy had gotten him kicked off the MIT project. Simply put, he'd created a program in which he detailed the political and economic history of a region, plugged in sociological factors past and present, along with a genetic profile of the inhabitants obtained from DNA studies, then ran them through the computer. With the collected data, the program, in theory, was then able to predict how any given population would respond under various circumstances.

There was another, darker side to his research that Hunter fully intended to keep under wraps. If the detailed DNA model he'd created fell into the wrong hands, it could theoretically be used to clone a genetically perfected warrior lacking in any social or moral conscience. An assassin class.

While he disliked working with bureaucrats, Hunter wasn't in any position to turn down much-needed funds. He'd always eschewed the money-raising circuit, but after that incident in Bosnia that had cost him half his face and a hand, he figured hostesses wouldn't exactly consider him a plus at their fund-raising dinners or cocktail parties.

His current work was being funded by both the State and Defense Departments, Defense wanting the data in order to predict wars and to discover how to map winning battle strategies, while State was seeking to defuse international skirmishes before they blew up into full-scale wars.

"I still have some work to do," he said obliquely. "The Middle East, for example, is still problematic."

They also didn't like him in that part of the world. He'd been shot at more times than he cared to think about during his stay in the region. And although he liked most of the population personally, he'd been warned on more than one occasion that he was con-

sidered a traitor for including various warring factions
into his model. The trouble with that was that in too
many parts of the world, people viewed as traitors
tended to disappear. Or get blown up.

Hunter hoped like hell that he wouldn't have to
return to Lebanon anytime soon. Beirut might have
once been the Paris of the region, but there were still
neighborhoods that could only be described as shoot-
ing galleries.

Then there was Kosovo. Hunter sighed. Good luck
keeping any negotiated peace in that place. And Bosnia. And Afghanistan. The list went on and on, and
while he had uncharacteristically high hopes for the
project, Hunter was also pragmatic enough to know
that trying to halt any outbreaks of violence around
the world was akin to attempting to plug a hole in
Hoover Dam with a finger.

"The powers that be are getting impatient," Van
Horn warned.

"Tough. The work will be done when it's done.
And not a minute before."

"They have to justify the expenditures to the
budget committee. I doubt you'd enjoy being the tar-
get of a congressional investigation."

Hunter lifted a brow. "Is that a threat?"

"Merely an observation."

"My budget is chicken feed compared to the bucks
you guys spend. Hell, the price of your expense account lunches at all those high-priced trendy Washington restaurants alone could fund me for another
six months.

"And if there do happen to be any mumblings
about expenditures up on the Hill, then it's your job

to quiet them. You guys aren't the only game in town, you know.''

A scowl darkened Van Horn's classically handsome WASP face. ''Then the other rumor about you meeting with the Russians is also true?''

''I haven't met with them.'' And wouldn't. But Hunter had perversely enjoyed the momentary panic he'd viewed in Van Horn's eyes. ''But I have received some inquiries regarding certain aspects of the project.''

''You realize that sharing information with them— especially information that's been classified—could get you arrested for treason.''

''I'll keep that in mind.''

Van Horn gave him another hard look, as if trying to determine whether or not Hunter was jerking his chain. Which, of course, he was. It was one of the few side benefits of working with bureaucrats. They were so marvelously predictable. And competitive.

''There's something else.'' Van Horn had begun working that crease again, Hunter noted.

''I rather suspected there might be.'' After all, a blizzard had been predicted and Hunter didn't figure the guy had come all the way to Castle Mountain to sip hot toddies beside a roaring fire at the Gray Gull inn and watch the winter wonderland occurring outside the lace-curtained windows.

''I heard from one of my sources at the CIA that you're on a terrorist hit list.''

''Why don't you tell me something I don't know?''

''I just wanted to pass the warning along.''

''Consider it passed.'' Hunter stood up, effectively ending what had turned out to be little more than a fishing expedition. ''And now that I've been properly

warned about Congress and terrorists, I'm sure you
won't mind if I return to work. After all,'' he said as
he plucked the soft cashmere coat from the rack and
held it out to James Van Horn, ''as you've pointed
out on so many other visits, time is money.''

With that he ushered the dapper diplomat out the
door. Then, giving up on getting any work done when
he couldn't keep his mind off the damn clock, he
locked the door to his inner office, set the secret code
on the security system, then headed home to wait for
Gillian's arrival.

FIVE DAYS AFTER her father's incredible revelation,
Gillian was sitting in the back of a car crawling its
way up the cliff leading out of the quaint village that
could be used as a movie set of a late-nineteenth century New England fishing village. The narrow gravel
road, which was currently packed with crunchy snow,
would soon become impassable for days during winter storms. Which was, Gillian thought, probably just
the way Hunter liked it.

All the articles she'd read about him, including the
recent one in *Newsweek,* invariably mentioned his ob-
sessively reclusive lifestyle these past years. Which
wasn't that surprising. She remembered how reluctantly he'd always seemed to attend the parties at her
parents' home. Even back then no one could have
called Hunter a social animal.

Of course, that hadn't stopped her mother from inviting him. And on those rare occasions when Hunter
would accept one of her invitations, Irene Cassidy
would pull out all the stops. She'd fluff her frosted
hair, and her skirts would be shorter, her necklines
lower.

Her eyes would become visibly brighter, glittering with a dangerous light, her silvery laugh would edge a few notes higher and several decimals louder, and the way her hips swayed as she walked in those high, spindly heels and tight skirts was guaranteed to draw the eye of every male in the room.

At the time Gillian had resented her mother's blatant sexuality. How in the world was Hunter ever going to notice her, a skinny adolescent with a mouthful of braces, when her mother was always flitting around him, like some exotic, gilded butterfly?

Unfortunately, the sad, miserable truth was that even without the competition from her mother, she could have been invisible where Hunter was concerned.

But apparently that had recently changed. According to her father, after viewing her recent video, Hunter had decided that he wanted to go to bed with her. Even knowing that as a modern, liberated woman of the twenty-first century, she should be appalled and infuriated by such a hideously outdated, chauvinistic attitude, there was just enough of that lovesick twelve-year-old still living inside Gillian to have her experience a warm flush of feminine satisfaction.

Not that she intended to actually sleep with Hunter, of course. The idea was as impossible as it was outrageous.

They came to a pair of tall wrought-iron gates topped with what appeared to be deadly iron spears. The driver paused beside a stone pillar. A moment later his window rolled down and he was touching a keypad. A camera hidden inside the gate whirred and there was a series of clicks. The gate slid smoothly open, allowing them access.

When they repeated that process three more times, Gillian decided that *reclusive* wasn't a strong-enough word to describe Hunter St. John. *Paranoid* might be a better fit, she thought as she realized that the camera was actually measuring and reading the driver's eye. She'd heard of such technology, but had never seen it firsthand.

The numerous security checks they passed through had Gillian expecting Hunter to live in a huge, hulking stone stronghold reminiscent of a medieval fortress. When they turned a final corner and the house came into view, she drew in a sharp, appreciative breath.

Constructed of cedar logs that had been aged to a pale, grayish blue, the house was perched like a seabird on the very edge of a cliff, offering spectacular views in every direction.

"Oh, it's absolutely stunning," she murmured to the driver, who, in the taciturn way of New Englanders, hadn't uttered more than five words during their choppy ride from the mainland.

"Ayuh," the man who'd introduced himself as Ben Adams agreed. "That's what most people say, first time they see it."

"I can imagine."

Actually, *stunning* didn't even begin to describe this architectural wonder. The focal point of the home was a two story glass wall that boldly thrust out from beneath the wooden-shake roof like the prow of a ship. Gillian imagined that standing next to that window must give the viewer a bird's-eye view of the stormy Atlantic. Two single-story wings jutted out from each side. Behind the house, pine trees rose like shaggy arrows shawled in white velvet.

"'Course, one of these days this cliff's gonna erode," the driver pointed out with Yankee practicality. "Then all St. John's gonna have left will be a pile of logs on the beach."

"In the meantime, he has a magnificent view," she said.

He shrugged. "Can't argue with that."

He pulled up into the curving driveway, stopping just in front of the double doors. "My missus works here during the week," he revealed, stringing together more words than he'd managed thus far. "She'll be inside, getting things ready for you. Dr. St. John said to expect you earlier," he volunteered. "By yesterday, at the latest."

"I was held up."

"That's what my missus told him probably happened." He parked the car. By the time he came around to open her door, she was already standing on the flagstone drive. "But Dr. St. John t'weren't too happy when last night came and you t'weren't here."

"I take it Dr. St. John is accustomed to having things his way?"

"Ayuh. That he is," Ben agreed. "But he's still a fair man to work for. When my Mildred came down with flu last winter, he paid her for days she couldn't even work."

Gillian was unimpressed by that little newsflash. "Gracious," she drawled, her voice thick with uncharacteristic sarcasm. "I'm surprised he wasn't voted the humanitarian of the year award for such an outstanding act of generosity."

He squinted down at her, obviously curious as to her reason for being here on the island in early December. From the icy wind blowing off the water,

Gillian suspected this wasn't exactly tourist season on Castle Mountain.

"He's a fair man," he repeated. "You'll find that out when you're working with him."

Gillian wondered what the elderly man would say if she told him the truth: that she wasn't here to work with Hunter, but had instead been ordered to Maine as part of his blackmail threat against her father.

He wouldn't believe her. Gillian didn't believe it herself. If she had, she never would have agreed to such a bizarre situation. Deep down inside, she continued to believe that Hunter's sole motivation was to shake her father's comfortable world to its foundations. Which he'd clearly done.

Now, having succeeded in watching his former mentor squirm, Gillian expected Hunter to laugh at her foolish naiveté and send her home. And that would be that.

The man she remembered might be unorthodox. But he wasn't cruel or dangerous. Surely human nature couldn't change that much?

Ben Adams's wife was tall and thin, with salt-and-pepper hair pulled back into a utilitarian knot at the nape of her long neck.

"Dr. St. John expected you earlier," she said as her husband carried Gillian's bags into the house.

"As a scientist, Dr. St. John should be accustomed to practicing patience."

Mildred Adams gave Gillian a long, hard look. "You're different from the other."

"The other?"

The husband and wife exchanged a brief glance. From the silent conversation that passed between them, Gillian guessed that Ben was cautioning discretion, while Mildred was determinedly outspoken.

Mildred's pale blue eyes took a long, judicious study, but she didn't directly answer Gillian's question. "Hope you're tougher than you look."

Gillian met the probing look with a level gaze of her own. "I've had to be."

That earned another hard look. "So has Dr. St. John. This could be interesting."

"Sorta like nitroglycerin and a flamethrower are interesting," her husband muttered. "Where do you want me to put these bags?"

"Dr. St. John said to put Ms. Cassidy in his room." She turned to Gillian, seemingly oblivious to the burn of embarrassment Gillian felt rise in her cheeks at the idea of this elderly couple believing she'd be sharing a bed with their employer. "I'll show you where it is. Then you can wash up for supper. I always serve at six o'clock, on the dot. Right before I leave for the day.

"Dr. St. John always eats in his laboratory. But he's instructed me to set a place for you in the dining room."

"He won't be eating with me?" Gillian asked as she followed the woman down the hallway.

"Oh, no. Dr. St. John is working at home this afternoon, but I doubt if you'll be seein' him until along about midnight, at the very earliest. When he gets busy with his experiments, it's like pulling teeth to drag him out of his lab." She handed Gillian an envelope. "I was instructed to give you this soon as you arrived. I expect it'll explain everything."

That said, the housekeeper opened one of two doors leading into what was obviously the master bedroom suite. The walls were constructed of the same logs as the rest of the house, but in here they'd been stained a lustrous golden brown. They were also, Gillian noted, the only warm thing about the room.

Decorated in shades of black and gray, with lots of jet lacquer and glass, the bedroom had an edgy, avant-garde look. More suitable for a modern art museum or a Fifth Avenue penthouse, it was decidedly too cold and remote for this gloriously wild place.

A huge bed, covered in a slick ebony spread, took up the center of the room. Gillian glanced up, cringing as she viewed the mirror over the bed.

Both Ben and Mildred studiously ignored both the mirror and Gillian's involuntary reaction to it.

"The bath's in there," Mildred said, pointing toward an arched doorway where an oversize Jacuzzi tub sat invitingly on a black-lacquered pedestal in front of a window. The wide expanse of triple-paned glass looked out over the darkening waters of the sea. "Dr. St. John had me clean out that bureau for your clothes." She waved her hand in the direction of a tall chest of drawers that matched the pedestal.

"I've got to serve and get on my way," Mildred continued briskly. "So, if you'll just get your washing-up done, I'll show you the way to the dining room."

"If I'm going to be eating alone, the kitchen will be fine," Gillian assured her.

"Dr. St. John said the dining room."

"And Dr. St. John always gets what Dr. St. John wants," Gillian muttered, beginning to get a handle on how things worked around here.

"Best you remember that," Mildred said with a brief, decisive nod. "The man's a good employer.

He's demanding. But fair,'' she said, echoing what her husband had told Gillian earlier. "Even so, I wouldn't want to cross him.''

And that, Gillian told herself ten minutes later, was why she was sitting all alone at a table designed to comfortably seat twelve. On some distant level she realized that the hearty corn chowder, green salad and brown bread was delicious, but although she hadn't eaten since boarding the plane in San Francisco, she couldn't work up any appetite for Mildred Adams's dinner. Not after reading Hunter's letter.

No, she considered, taking another sip of the red wine she'd found waiting at her place, it wasn't really a letter. It was more an instruction manual.

Written in a bold scrawl, it had begun without pre-amble.

> Gillian,
> Welcome to Castle Mountain. I trust you will enjoy your time here on the island and that when you leave you will take fond memories with you.

Her mistake had been, of course, allowing those words to soften her, to make her able to believe that this trip to Maine was nothing more than a well-deserved vacation after her grueling tour.

The next paragraph proved otherwise, bringing home with a vengeance the true reason for her being here on this remote island. In this even more remote house.

> You'll find a gown on the bed. After you bathe, put it on. Wear your hair down, and if you're wearing makeup, take it off. The image I want

you to project is the one from your concert at Stonehenge—pure and innocent, yet with that aura of untapped sensuality surrounding you.

I'll be working late, but I expect you to remain awake until I join you in the bedroom. I trust the next month will be enjoyable for both of us.

However, if you find my demands not quite to your taste, just remember, if you leave before the thirty days are up, I will, without a moment's hesitation, ruin your father.

The choice is yours, lovely Gillian. I trust your arrival here, albeit a day late, reveals your willingness to accede to my wishes. Whatever they may be.

It was signed merely with a dark *H*.

"Damn."

Gillian cursed yet again as she stared out into the well of darkness. It was a new moon; the sky and water were both pitch black, extending for what seemed forever.

For the first time since her arrival on the remote island, her isolation, along with what she'd foolishly agreed to, came crashing down on her.

Hunter had promised he would not hurt her. But what if he was lying? What if he was as cold and unfeeling as his hateful letter?

After all, she reminded herself, what kind of man could even think up such a scenario in the first place? What if he planned to literally hold her captive, using her in ways too horrific even to imagine?

The scenario—the virgin sent to some remote lair to pay off her father's debt—could have come straight from the pages of some lurid melodrama.

"Damn you, Father."

Her flare of anger was immediately followed by a heavy sense of despair. And impending doom.

"Oh, God," she murmured. "What have I done?"

So, HUNTER THOUGHT as he watched her on the monitor in his book-lined office. *It's finally sunk in. Good.*

He'd watched her enter the house as if she were merely arriving at some ritzy seaside spa where she expected to be pampered and perfumed, wrapped in mud and dine on pretty little salads made from flowers. He hadn't missed the derision on her fragile, porcelain-pale face as she'd looked up at his mirror.

The brief flashes of self-assurance she'd displayed to Mildred and Ben Adams suggested that Cassidy had been telling the truth about one thing. The woman did have a mind of her own. Which, he considered, made her even more of a challenge.

He'd promised Cassidy that he wouldn't harm her. Which was true. But Hunter did have every intention of spending the next thirty nights bending Gillian to his will, teaching her things about herself, revealing the dark, forbidden secret corners of her sexual psyche he suspected she'd never known existed.

Her display of self-pity turned out to be short-lived. Hunter watched as she cursed—a rich, earthy word that drew a faint smile from him. She threw her napkin onto the table, stood up and left the room.

The hall camera caught her flashing eyes and firmly set lips as she strode purposefully back toward the master suite.

Oh, yes, Hunter told himself, his body humming with savage anticipation, the ethereal-appearing pianist's surprisingly independent spirit would only make their little game more intriguing.

And it would definitely make his victory all the sweeter once George Cassidy's daughter had been properly, thoroughly tamed.

THE STAGE IN THE MASTER suite had been set for seduction. The flames coming from the fire in the black-tiled fireplace warming the bedroom were in stark contrast to the icy sleet the ocean wind was driving against the windowpanes.

The flickering orange light danced on the ceiling like a shimmering display of aurora borealis. On the table beside the bed, a fat ivory beeswax candle sat on a hammered-tin holder.

The nightgown—a pale sea-foam green rather than the blatant black she'd been expecting—was draped across the bed, just as Hunter's insulting letter had promised. Since it hadn't been there earlier, and Mr. and Mrs. Adams had left right after Mildred had served dinner, Hunter had obviously left his precious laboratory long enough to lay it out for her.

The idea of his prowling unseen through the sprawling house, entering her room, perhaps even going through her personal belongings, gave Gillian goose bumps.

It also made her madder than hell.

The gown was empire style, the top created from hand-tatted lace so gossamer it could have been spun by fairies from cobwebs. In spite of her pique and determination not to fall into the sensual trap he'd set, Gillian was unwillingly drawn to the delicate fabric.

She lifted it off the bed and ran her fingertips over the lacy rosettes designed to cover her breasts. The center of the flowers had been left open, obviously designed to bare a woman's nipples.

"Yet more proof that subtlety isn't the man's strong suit," she muttered. The material might be exquisite, but the style was Frederick's of Hollywood. There was no way she was going to wear this, Gillian decided firmly. She glared up at the mirror over her head.

"Not until we set a few ground rules, first."

HUNTER LAUGHED at her declaration. A rough, humorous bark that echoed in the cavernous confines of his laboratory. The room was dark, illuminated only by the faint icy sparkle of stars outside the wall of glass and the glow coming from the computer monitor and bank of television screens.

"Brave talk, little one," he murmured, lifting the balloon glass of cognac in a silent salute. "But words won't help you. Not now."

He watched her scowl soften as her fingertips absently traced the lacy flowers. Women were so marvelously predictable, he thought with masculine satisfaction. He'd often wondered why men claimed to be mystified by the female mind.

All you had to do was to experience enough of them to create a workable model, program in the data, and they'd behave exactly as expected, at least ninety-two percent of the time. The eight percent of their behavior that could admittedly prove unpredictable had never disturbed him. It was, Hunter had determined long ago, what kept them from becoming boring.

"You're tempted, Gillian," he said to the screen. "Try the gown on. You know you want to."

He watched as she closed her eyes and smoothed her hand over the sensuous silk.

"That's it. Feel how smooth it is. Imagine it against your bare skin, sliding down your body like a cool waterfall."

As if in response to his crooned command, Gillian opened her eyes and slipped her hand between the layers of silk. Then, in a seemingly hypnotic gesture, she lifted the gown against her body and slowly turned toward the full-length mirror standing in the corner of the room.

She was still clad in the somber charcoal-gray sweater and tweed slacks she'd worn on the flight to Maine. Yet it took no imagination for Hunter to imagine her nude. She was holding the gown with her right hand; her left began slowly trailing over the shimmering sea-foam silk.

Hunter pressed the remote to zoom in on a closeup and watched as a breath slipped from between Gillian's parted pink lips. It was little more than a whisper, but the microphone in the bedroom had no trouble picking it up. Hunger suddenly had claws.

Needing to touch something—someone—Hunter thrust his hand beneath his sweater, splayed his right palm across his hot, burning chest and felt the increased beat of his heart beneath his fingertips.

As he watched Gillian's exploring hand move slowly downward, his body came fully to life, pressing painfully against the hard barrier of denim that was a poor substitute for a woman's hand. Struck with an almost overwhelming urge to yank open his jeans and satisfy the woman hunger that was ripping away at him—as it had for too many nights lately—Hunter decided the time had come to personally welcome his alluring houseguest to Castle Mountain.

THE NIGHTGOWN WAS COOL and seductively sensual to the touch. It was also nearly transparent. A woman wearing this gown would be revealing far more than merely her body, Gillian feared. She'd be putting her inner self on display, as well.

Even as she fought against it, some compulsion she was unable to resist made her hold the gown against her body. She drew in a sharp breath at her reflection. Even though she was fully dressed beneath the silk, the transformation proved riveting.

Her eyes seemed strangely wider and burned with the same edgy brilliance Gillian remembered seeing in her mother's gaze whenever Irene Cassidy had been preparing to welcome Hunter to her husband's house. There was an unfamiliar, almost painful tightening in her breasts. And between her legs.

"It suits you."

Not having heard him approach, the deep voice made Gillian jump. She dropped the gown and pressed a palm against her pounding heart as she whirled around and viewed Hunter standing in the open doorway.

4

HUNTER WAS IN THE SHADOWS, which precluded her from getting a good look at him. But he seemed even larger than Gillian remembered. And far more menacing. In his black sweater and black jeans, he reminded her of a creature of the night.

She pressed a hand against her breast where her runaway heart was beating like a terrified rabbit's.

"You scared me to death!"

"I don't know why. You knew I was in the house. I informed you in my note that I'd be joining you in my room after supper. You should have been expecting me."

"Mrs. Adams said you didn't usually leave your lab until after midnight."

"Since Mrs. Adams has never stayed a minute past six in the three years she's been employed here, I have no idea how she'd be cognizant of my work habits."

He crossed the room, moving with a dangerous, stealthy grace, bent down and plucked the gown from the floor. "You aren't dressed."

Wary, but refusing to admit it, Gillian lifted her chin and met his gaze. It took every ounce of self-control she possessed not to gasp at the sight of the twisted scars marring the left side of the face she'd never quite been able to get out of her mind. Or the glint of the firelight flickering on what could only be described as a hook that had taken the place of his left hand.

She swallowed and kept her expression cool when what she longed to do was weep for whatever tragedy had befallen him. "Actually, I am dressed."

His firmly cut lips twisted into a mockery of a smile that revealed not the faintest glimmer of humor. If the eyes were indeed windows to the soul, Hunter's reminded her of storm shutters painted black.

It had been too long since he'd had a haircut; his shaggy jet hair, curling around his collar, was as unruly as his reputation. He also hadn't shaved; the dark shadow on the still-unscarred side of his face added to his dangerously uncivilized appearance.

Gillian was a little afraid of him. She was even more afraid of herself. And the reckless, crazy way he was making her feel. Even as she felt a sharp tingle of misgiving, her fingers practically itched with the need to touch that roughened red flesh.

The desire to soothe warred with the old childhood taboo against revealing impolite fascination with any sort of disfigurement or handicap. And both those emotions battled with the unbidden feminine awareness that was humming through her veins.

"You're still in your traveling clothes," he said mildly. "I instructed you to wear this." He held the nightgown toward her.

The contrast between the delicate pastel silk and the cold steel caused a distinct twinge somewhere deep in her feminine core. With the exception of her music, Gillian had always been a woman who'd ruled her emotions—rather than letting them rule her. That being the case, she reminded herself about her determination to set some ground rules to this strange game Hunter had brought her here to play.

"I thought it might be a nice idea if we could have a chance to talk, first."

"You don't seem to understand."

Apparently deciding not to push the issue of the gown for now, he sat down in a black suede tub chair. He was no longer towering over her, but when he stretched his long legs out in front of him, spreading them open to reveal his blatant arousal, Gillian felt no less threatened. And even more emotionally rattled.

"There's nothing for us to talk about," he said.

"We could begin with hello."

He sighed heavily. Wearily. "Hello." The word was offered without a hint of welcome. His hooded eyes flicked over her—appraising, assessing. "You've grown up."

"I suppose that's inevitable. Since I was twelve years old the last time you saw me."

"That's why I barely remembered you."

He had no way of knowing exactly how badly those words stung. A distinctly feminine part of her bridled at the unflattering remark.

"Well, no one could accuse you of trying to get a woman into bed by boosting her ego."

"Would you rather I lie and tell you that I'd found you incredibly desirable back then? That thinking about you made me hot? That I laid awake nights, getting hard as I fantasized what it would feel like to strip that ugly schoolgirl uniform off your body and touch your soft, white, virginal, adolescent flesh all over?''

''Of course I wouldn't have wanted you to notice me in that way,'' she said, surprising herself by her ability to speak so calmly after his sarcastic words had slapped her as badly as if he'd struck her. Her fantasies, which may have admittedly been heightened by a bit of sexual desire she hadn't understood at the time had always been of a gilded romantic nature, as if filmed with a soft-focus lens. ''The very idea is disgusting.''

''On that we can agree. Believe me, sweetheart, the only females who have ever turned me on are well past the age of consent.''

''Like my mother.'' The words were out of her mouth before she could stop them. Horrified, Gillian would have done anything to be able to call them back.

Hunter didn't immediately respond. Instead, he treated her to another examination, this one longer, more intimate, starting at the top of her head, moving with tantalizing slowness over her body, down to her boots, then back up again to her face.

He was measuring her, in a flagrantly masculine way that made her vividly aware of every inch of skin his gaze touched.

''Irene was a very appealing woman, in her way. But you, Gillian, have surpassed her.''

The compliment, offered without an iota of warmth from a man capable of making her feel hot and icy all at the same time, should not have given her any pleasure, Gillian told herself. It shouldn't. But, dammit, it did.

"Men have always found my mother sexually appealing."

Which was why, Gillian knew, she'd been sent away to boarding school before her fourteenth birthday. It was, after all, difficult to appear endlessly young with a teenager in the house.

"To tell the truth," Hunter said with a thoughtful frown, "Irene was always too obvious for my taste. She reminded me a lot of the moonshine we used to make in the lab in my undergraduate days—cheap, potent and capable of leaving a man with one helluva hangover afterward....

"Over the years I've come to prefer a smooth, complex cognac. The type that lingers on the tongue."

When his gaze drifted wickedly back down to her breasts, the butterflies that had been flapping their wings in Gillian's stomach turned to giant condors.

She decided the time had come to change the subject. To bring it back to her reason for having come to Castle Mountain island in the first place.

"My father told me about your threat to destroy him."

"I assumed as much. Since you're here."

He pulled the silk through the delicate prongs of the hook, absently stroking it with his good hand in a way that suggested he was already envisioning her wearing it. And taking it off her.

"What a loyal daughter you are, Gillian. And what a shame that George Cassidy doesn't deserve such a sacrifice."

He was so damn smug! So pleased with his ability to play with people, to move them around at his whim as if life was merely his own personal life-size chess-board.

Gillian tossed her head. "He also told me about your accusation."

His eyes narrowed as if she'd just called him a liar. "It happens to be the truth. And I can prove it."

There was no need. Gillian knew Hunter was telling the truth. "Why did you wait so long to do anything about it?" Her voice, no longer cool, wavered, revealing her distress with not only her personal situation, but her father's treachery.

"I don't suppose you'd believe that I was waiting for you to grow up?" he inquired whimsically.

Gillian was strangely grateful for his unemotional, almost distant tone. It helped her gather up her scattered composure. It also expunged any pity she might have been feeling concerning whatever tragedies he'd suffered since that day he'd stormed from the lab.

"Since you've already admitted to not remembering me, I'd find that explanation difficult to accept."

His careless shrug suggested he'd figured as much. "Surely you've heard that old saying about revenge being a dish best served cold?"

"That's all this is about? Revenge?"

"Can you think of a better reason?"

He was a disturbing man. A disturbing and fascinating man. Having only ever dated men of her own world—charming, unthreatening males who prided themselves on having moved beyond ancient chauvinistic male behavior—Gillian was finding Hunter's

cooly cynical attitude as compelling as it was un-
nerving.

"I'm not afraid of you," she said, not quite truth-
fully.

"You should be. You're also lying, which is
against the rules of our little game."

"I don't understand." She dragged her hand
through her hair again and as it settled back over her
shoulders, watched a hot desire that was as unsettling
as the rest of him flare in his midnight eyes. "Why
me?"

She'd never thought of herself as the type of
woman who instilled lustful thoughts. Even her music, which had been called "hot-tub Muzak" by its
detractors, was designed to soothe rather than excite.

"It's quite simple, Gillian. Something about your
Celtic video moved me. I can't explain it, but the fact
is, I want you. And I intend to have you."

"Do you always get everything you want?" she
asked with genuine curiosity.

He stood up and moved toward her. "Are you always this argumentative?"

He was suddenly too close. Gillian took an uncon-
scious step back. "Actually, most people find me
quite agreeable." She decided this was not the time
to mention the petulant male crew in Rio.

"Really?" He took another step. "Perhaps I bring
out the worst in you."

She could feel the heat from his body, but refusing
to give him the satisfaction of knowing exactly how
strongly he intimidated her, Gillian held her ground.

"Oh, I'd say that was a given," she said with mock
sweetness. She was not ordinarily sarcastic. But this

was, she reminded herself, a far from ordinary situation.

Hunter sighed and shook his head. "I don't understand. You were made aware of my intentions, and the fact that you're here in Castle Mountain, in my house, indeed, in my bedroom, would lead any reasonable man to conclude that you've agreed to my terms. So why do you suddenly feel the need to test my restraint?"

"I have no idea what you're talking about," she said, fudging the truth again, despite Hunter's prohibition against lying.

Despite the note, the nightgown, even the mirror overhead, Gillian still couldn't make herself believe that he could possibly be serious.

"There you go, breaking the rules again." His dark eyes were as confident as a predator who'd cornered his prey. "Of course you know what I'm referring to. The deal I made with your father was that your days would be your own. But your nights belong to me."

Hunter's wolfish smile radiated male arrogance. "Yet the sun has gone down, and here you are, still overdressed."

He frowned as he took in the expensive slacks and sweater she'd bought in Belfast, where she'd played to a full house three nights in a row at the Grand Opera House.

"If you were hoping I'd strip them off you, then have my wild, wicked way with you, I have to confess that rape has never been one of my fantasies.

"But you will take them off for me, Gillian," he assured her as his gleaming dark eyes glided over her.

"It may take a few minutes, or even a few hours, but you'll soon learn to obey my every command.

"If I tell you to lean over that chest so I can take you hard and fast from behind, you'll do it without question. If I instruct you to kneel on this floor and take me deep in your lovely mouth, you'll swallow me deeper than you've ever swallowed any other man without a murmur of protest. My game, Gillian. My rules."

There was a sinister timbre to his voice that caused pinpricks of anxiety to skim up her spine. But understanding that it was vital to establish her own position in this strange game he'd brought her here to play, Gillian struggled for some semblance of calm.

"This may come as a shock to your chauvinist nature, Hunter, but women in these enlightened times do not take orders from men."

"You will. And you know what, Gillian? You're going to love it. You'll obey me because you choose to, not because I make you do anything you won't willingly agree to."

Feeling rashly daring and defiant, she glared up at him. "I do wish you'd stop treating me like some prostitute you've bought for the night."

"I don't consider you a prostitute, Gillian. Although, in a way, I suppose, you could say I've booked your services. But for a great deal more than a single night."

Her hands curled into fists at her side as Gillian, who'd never hit another human being in her life, was suddenly tempted to slap him. With herculean effort, she resisted the uncharacteristic impulse. Just barely.

"My father was right." With him standing so

close, she had to tilt her head back to glare up at him. "You are a devil."

"That may be." Appearing unfazed by her insult, he rubbed his unshaven jaw, giving her the impression he was actually considering the idea. "Which means, I suppose, that you're soon going to discover exactly how it feels to dance—metaphorically speaking—with the devil."

He held out the nightgown again. His eyes were as hard and as dark as onyx, his lips set in a foreboding line. "Now, I want you free of all the artifices that cover your lovely body, Gillian. So, either you take off your clothes, or I'll do it for you. But if you lead me to do that, believe me, sweetheart, you'll never be able to wear them again."

She wondered what had happened to his so-called promise not to make her do anything she didn't want.

"I could leave."

"There's a new moon tonight. And even if you could get past the security gates, which believe me, you couldn't, the road down to the shore is treacherous enough in the daytime. In the dark it's deadly. You could fall off the cliff. And how could I ever explain your tragic demise to your loving father?"

His voice was thick with sarcasm. Even as she reminded herself that she'd been a very young impressionable girl when she'd known Hunter, Gillian couldn't believe that she was capable of so misjudging a man.

But then again, she considered grimly, hadn't she always believed that her father was an honorable man? And look how wrong she'd been about that.

"If you're planning to hit me, or whip me, or strike me in any way, I really am leaving."

"You needn't worry about that. I'm not into whips or chains."

"I also won't take part in any orgies." About this she was perfectly clear. "So if you're thinking about bringing any other players into this strange game of yours, I'd rather take my chances with the dark and the cliff."

"I suppose I could agree to that. So long as you prove yourself woman enough to satisfy me," he tacked on wickedly.

Bile rose in her throat at the idea that her entire life had once revolved around this man.

During those lonely teen years in Switzerland, she'd even kept a secret scrapbook filled with clippings about his successes after her father had forced him from MIT, including the articles about his genetic personality profile test, which, while as controversial as everything else about Hunter, had been embraced by businesses worldwide. It was undoubtedly those royalties that had paid for this luxurious house.

Even though she'd put the scrapbook away years ago, she'd continued to think about him more than was reasonable for a woman who should have outgrown a childhood crush by now.

"You truly are disgusting."

He shrugged, obviously unwounded. "The clothes, Gillian," he reminded her on a soft voice more deadly than the loudest shout. "I'd suggest beginning with the boots. And then we'll progress from there."

5

EVER SINCE HER FATHER had told her about Hunter's threat, Gillian had continued to assure herself that she wasn't really going to have sex with Hunter. Oh, once or twice the thought had crossed her mind that perhaps he truly was serious, and during those times, she'd managed to comfort herself that if necessary, to save her father, she could make herself go through with it. But now she couldn't move.

"All right." His voice twined around her like an ebony velvet cord. "I'll help you. This first time."

She pressed a hand against his chest. "Hunter. Don't do this."

He ignored her faint protest. "I like the way you say my name. In that throaty tone, with just a little hitch in your voice." He ran his fingertips along the cowl neckline of her sweater, creating a trail of sparks. Then pressed his thumb against the pulsing hollow at the base of her throat. "Are you afraid of me, Gillian?"

When she didn't—couldn't—answer, he slipped his fingers beneath the soft wool.

Having spent so many of her childhood years in a home devoid of affection, where even her mother's touches had been saved for men other than her husband, men like Hunter St. John, Gillian had never thought of herself as a physical person. Until now.

"You needn't be afraid." His deep voice was strangely hypnotic, like that of a dark angel leading her into dangerous temptation. "I told you, I promise not to do anything that you truly—deep down inside—don't want me to do."

His fingers were creating havoc to her nerve endings, making her feel as if she were standing on the very edge of the cliff outside the wall of glass, about to fling her body into the endless ebony void.

Without warning, he yanked the sweater over her head.

"I never would have taken you for a white cotton girl, Gillian," he murmured with a faint note of amusement as he eyed her utilitarian bra.

"Cotton's comfortable."

"It's also not the least bit erotic." Imprisoning both her wrists in his right hand, he released the front catch with a deft flick of the hook. "It reminds me of something a nun might wear to keep impure thoughts at bay. You won't wear this again while you're here."

"I would think I should be allowed to wear whatever I please," she murmured even as her heart beat faster. Harder. "At least, during the days you promised would be my own."

"I lied."

Seeming entranced with the paleness of her skin, he reached out and traced a slender blue vein from the wall of her chest to her left nipple. Then continued the sensual titillation on the other breast while watching her face for her reaction. Which, though she struggled not to show him, Gillian suspected was bordering on intoxication.

She couldn't decide who she was angrier with—Hunter for creating this outrageous scenario, or herself for having foolishly believed she could handle it.

Through the pounding of blood in her head, Gillian realized that she was standing on the edge of emotional quicksand. The trick, she realized as Hunter continued to batter away at her senses, was to escape before she sank in over her head.

She jerked away. "Dammit, Hunter, if you're going to insist I follow through with this ridiculous farce, could you please knock off the fake seduction routine and just get it over with?"

"It's no farce."

"Isn't it? Do you always have to blackmail women to get them into your bed?"

"No." He seemed almost amused by her continued defiance. "You're the first."

Unable to find anything remotely humorous about this situation, Gillian welcomed the anger stimulated by the sardonic quirk of his lips. It helped take her mind off the strange, unbidden burning, melting sensation caused by his wicked touch.

"I don't suppose you thought of trying some other more typical seduction tactic? Like sending flowers? Or inviting me to dinner?"

"I considered them. Especially since too many women seem to feel freer if they can wrap what's basically animal lust up into pretty, romanticized packages. But in your case, I chose to go with a more direct method.''

Gillian suspected that pretending romanticized feelings toward her would have also deprived him of what he'd really wanted—the pleasure of watching her father squirm when he'd tossed his outrageous proposition in the older man's face.

"Tell me, Gillian, if I had sent you baskets of hothouse red roses and gilded boxes of chocolate truffles, and even perhaps, penned flowery notes comparing your beauty to a summer's day, would you have gone to bed with me?''

"Not on a bet.'' All right. So perhaps it wasn't the absolute truth. Gillian was rapidly discovering that despite his horrid behavior, she was as susceptible to this man as she'd been all those years ago. Perhaps even more so, now that she understood those unnamed feelings she'd experienced.

A challenging silence stretched between them. The air in the bedroom became charged with sensuality.

"You know,'' Hunter said finally. "I believe I'll change the rules to our little game.''

"Now, why doesn't that surprise me?''

He shook his head and clucked his tongue. "This unfortunate habit you have of responding with sarcasm to my attempts at conversation—conversation you said you wanted,'' he reminded her, "is going to have to stop. Right now.''

She tensed, momentarily afraid that he was going to renege on his promise not to strike her. But instead, he released her, went over to where Ben Adams had left her luggage, unzipped the smaller of the two bags, found the compartment where she'd packed her underwear and scooped it up. Gillian was shocked when he took the unadorned panties and bras and threw them in the fireplace.

"You can't do that!"

"My game, my rules. I can do anything I want, remember?" he asked on a silky, threatening tone that both unnerved and aroused her.

While she watched in stunned shock as flames scorched her panties and bras, he walked over to the dresser, opened a drawer and retrieved a pile of brightly hued silk and satin lingerie that reminded her of a treasure trove of purloined jewels.

"I suppose those were confiscated from other members of your harem?" she asked dryly.

"George was right," he murmured. "Not only do you have a mind of your own, you're obviously not afraid to speak it."

"If you want a silent lover you can bend to your every will, I'd suggest a blowup doll," she suggested with saccharine sweetness.

Hunter appeared unwounded by her insult. "I think I'd rather join an order of Trappist monks than resort to that. And as it happens, I bought all this for you."

"Oh." Although she'd never indulged in fancy lingerie, Gillian found the sight of those lace confections as undeniably seductive as the nightgown. "I have difficulty picturing you shopping at Victoria's Secret."

"You'd be surprised what you can buy on the Internet these days."

"Surely you're not going to burn them, too?" He

wouldn't. Then she realized that she was no longer certain about anything concerning this man.

There was another long pause, during which Hunter studied the colorful lingerie, seeming to honestly consider that idea.

"No," he decided finally. "I don't think so. Perhaps we'll find a use for them later." His smile was vibrant with sexual insinuation. "Much, much later...

"In the meantime, I'm beginning to come to the reluctant conclusion that you're too sexually repressed, Gillian. Which, I'll have to admit is a revelation, since your music suggests that you're a woman of great passion.

"And while I'd planned a great many erotic pleasures for your first night in my home, I believe we'll have to slow the timetable a bit."

He dropped the bits of silk and satin onto the mattress, where they looked like confetti, then came to stand in front of her again. The long dark fingers of his right hand cupped her breast.

Then, while his eyes held hers with the sheer strength of masculine will, he slowly lowered his head until his mouth was a mere breath away from hers.

"Feel how your body warms to my touch, Gillian," he murmured, his words feathering across her lips like a soft summer breeze. She could smell the cognac he'd mentioned earlier on his breath. He lifted her breast and kissed the pale crevice beneath it, causing her heart to leap beneath his lips.

"I could drag you down to the floor and take you right now. And then, while you were still trembling from the strongest orgasm of your life, I could make you come again. And again, all night long. I could give you the best sex of your life, Gillian. And leave you begging for more.''

His words, along with the raw hunger glittering in his eyes, conspired to make Gillian feel needy. And confused. Her memories of Hunter had always been wrapped in the misty gauze of an adoring adolescent's fantasy. She never would have believed that such a crude description could make every nerve in her body thrum.

She realized that her conflicted feelings were binding her to Hunter—and to this unsettling sexual scenario—as inexorably as a pair of velvet handcuffs might bind her to his bed.

Gillian was trying to think of something, anything to say, when his head swooped down and his mouth captured hers in a rough, searing assault that took her breath away.

Like his words, meant to shock and arouse her, there was no subtlety to the savage kiss. His lips ground against hers, his unshaven jaw felt like sandpaper against her skin, his teeth punished. He thrust his tongue between her teeth, plunging deeply.

Both hand and hook tangled in her hair and dragged her head back, taking the kiss deeper, darker, devouring her.

Then, when her head was swimming and her bones felt as if they were melting from the inside out, the devastating kiss ended as swiftly as it had begun.

''You've had a long flight. A long day,'' he said. ''We'll continue this tomorrow.''

Gillian stared up at Hunter through the lingering

fog of unwilling desire, trying to make sense of his words. But confused and shaken as she was, he could have been speaking a foreign language.

"I don't understand what you want from me."

"What do I want, lovely Gilly?"

He ran the back of his hand down her cheek in a long sweep that started her trembling all over again. His gaze, which had turned remote, was no less compelling.

"Everything."

With that ominous declaration, he scooped up the lingerie from the bed and left the room.

The whips she'd feared earlier could not have hurt Gillian as much as his sudden detachment. What kind of man could turn from flame to ice in the blink of an eye? His game, she reminded herself bleakly.

Shaken to the core, Gillian sank down on the mattress, put her hand to her head, closed her eyes and took several deep breaths. Then buried her face in her hands and tried not to weep.

SHE WAS STILL SITTING there looking even more fragile and vulnerable when Hunter returned. He stood in the doorway and took in the sight of her, sitting on his wide empty bed, her lovely face covered by those long pianist's fingers.

Something that felt uncomfortably like guilt stirred and was immediately restrained.

Gillian Cassidy was a grown woman, Hunter reminded himself. No one had forced her to come here to Castle Mountain. She'd come of her free will, understanding that for the next thirty nights she would be at his command, for him to use in whatever way he wanted, for his pleasure.

But she'd be pleasured, too. Beyond her wildest imagination. It was obvious that despite the ugly underwear, she was as much a sexual adventuress as Toni. Why else, he asked himself, would she have agreed to his demands?

The moment his mouth had captured hers, Hunter had felt the shock followed by a momentous fear rock through Gillian. Then, as she'd given herself over to sexual sensation of his tongue embracing hers, teasing it into a dance of compliance, he'd felt her surrender.

That single kiss had confirmed what her music had suggested: beneath that innocent facade, hidden fires smoldered. Hunter suspected it would not take much to fan those flames into a conflagration.

So why, he wondered, did she seem so damn distressed? So lost?

He watched her rub at her temples with trembling fingers, as if to soothe the wildness he'd planted in her mind, and felt a strange, uncharacteristic urge to stroke her hair or even, perhaps, to offer some words of comfort.

Hunter had wanted Gillian from the first moment he'd seen her video. That sharp tug of desire hadn't particularly disturbed him; he'd wanted women before. Before that letter bomb had nearly killed him, he'd enjoyed an active and varied sex life. He'd certainly never felt any need to apologize for being male and human.

But never had any woman taken such hold of his mind the way this woman had. He thought about her during the day, when he should be working; he dreamed about her during the night, when he should be sleeping. And he couldn't even count the times he'd watched that damn Celtic concert tape.

If all that wasn't bad enough, there was the little fact that never in his life had he ever needed a woman like he needed Gillian at this moment.

Which was why Hunter had decided it would be wise to step back—literally and figuratively—from this potentially volatile situation.

Uneasy at the tug of unfamiliar emotion, he entered the room, pulled her hand away from her forehead, then pressed a glass into it with more pressure than necessary.

"I brought you something to help you sleep."

Gillian slowly opened her eyes and frowned suspiciously at the small white tablet he was holding out to her.

"I don't take sleeping pills. Drugs always make me feel too groggy the next day."

"It's not a drug. It's herbal and completely safe. I've used it myself, on occasion in the past, to prevent jet lag."

"I never get jet lag."

"And you probably always sleep like a baby, too. But why don't you take it, just the same?" The suggestion was swathed in silk, but no less an order.

"I suppose if I don't, you'll just thrust it down my throat." Dammit, her voice—frail, fractured and needy—strummed countless unnamed chords inside Hunter.

"I told you, Gillian," he replied with a patience he

was currently a very long way from feeling. "You won't have to do anything you don't want to do."

What he wanted was her surrender. Her absolute submission, given freely. Fortunately, in his years as a research scientist he had acquired patience. While it wasn't his first choice, he could wait.

"But you've had a long day, a grueling flight, you're going to be sleeping in a strange bed and you can deny it all you want, but you're every bit as stimulated by me as I am by you."

Giving into impulse, he ran his palm down the rippling red-gold waves tumbling over her bare shoulders.

"We're going to be a perfect match, Gillian. Together we're going to do things you've never done, things you never could have dreamed you wanted done to you. I'm going to push you beyond what you've always believed to be your sexual limits, then have you begging for more. We're going to free you, Gillian. Free you from the veil of repression you seem to have donned like a nun's habit. Then I'll bring you with me, naked, into the fire."

His hand slid beneath the silk of her hair; his fingers massaged the nape of her neck. "But you can put your concerns away, at least for tonight."

He stood up and looked down at her, aroused by the lingering sensuality smoldering in her eyes. Thunder rumbled through his cock even as his heart was oddly and uncomfortably touched by the apprehension he viewed in those gentle green depths.

He wanted to touch her one more time, but because it was imperative that he maintain control over this situation—over her and himself—Hunter refused to give in to the almost overwhelming urge.

"You'll dream of me."

He flashed her a wicked, practiced grin, then turned and walked out of the bedroom again, away from temptation.

THE FOLLOWING MORNING Gillian grumpily decided that Hunter must be some sort of evil erotic wizard. Because, just as he'd promised, she did, indeed, dream of him. Hot, vividly sensual dreams that left the lush Egyptian cotton sheets hopelessly tangled and had her waking with her hand between her legs, her body aching with unsatiated need.

She hadn't been lying when she'd told Hunter that she never got jet lag. Fortunately, she'd always been one of those people for whom sleep came easily. Whether on a plane, in the back of a taxi, or in a strange bed in a foreign hotel room thousands of miles from home, she could drop off in an instant, doze for ten minutes, or sleep for six hours, and awake feeling renewed and rested.

This made touring, while admittedly rigorous, less of a nightmare for her than for other performers. She could easily be on a concert stage at midnight and have no trouble arriving at the airport early the next morning feeling fresh and ready to tackle another day.

But during her first night in Castle Mountain not only had her sleep been restless, she didn't awaken until nearly noon. Horribly groggy, she managed to drag herself into the bathroom adjoining the luxurious bedroom suite.

Although she tried not to even look at the Jacuzzi, it was difficult to avoid it, holding center stage as it did. For a fleeting moment her mind conjured up a fantasy of lying naked in Hunter's arms while warm jets of water bubbled around them.

"Safe herbal sleep remedy, ha," she muttered, turning on the shower with a vicious twist of the wrist.

The tile-and-glass cubicle filled with steam as Gillian stood beneath the needles of hot water, scrubbing viciously at her skin. After her shower, she wrapped herself in the thick robe hanging nearby. The robe enveloped her like a warm black cocoon.

She knew instantly that it was Hunter's. He'd worn it recently; she ran her hand absently down the lapel as she breathed in his scent.

Gillian had never considered herself a very sexual person, which was how she'd managed to reach the age of twenty-five a virgin. Having witnessed her mother's constant affairs and escapades, she'd made the decision long ago to never take sex lightly.

Her mother had lost a great deal—her home, her husband, her daughter—because of her sad, desperate need to be desired. Watching Irene Cassidy's hedonistic, yet at the same time self-destructive behavior over the years, Gillian had come to the conclusion that sex equaled surrender. The simple truth was that she'd never met a man she'd been tempted to relinquish control to.

Until now.

Hunter obviously possessed a strong, earthy nature. He was also completely amoral, making her wonder what had happened to that high-principled young man she'd once adored from afar. It was obvious that he'd undergone some physical tragedy.

Even worse than his visible scars was the apparent loss of his heart. And even, she feared, his soul.

In another time, he would have been considered a sexual libertine—a man without conscience who seduced women for his own amusement, abandoning them without a backward glance once he grew bored with the game.

Of course, the women would know they were being seduced, Gillian allowed. And even those who tried to resist the sensual lure of his mocking bedroom eyes, his dark voice with its menacing shadow of sensuality, would understand that this was a game they couldn't win.

Nevertheless, perhaps because he represented the forbidden, the dark side of human nature, since arriving on Castle Mountain Island, Gillian was discovering how the lure of capitulation to such a man could prove irresistible.

6

HUNTER WAS IN A FILTHY MOOD. He'd spent the night chasing sleep, his mutinous mind filled with images of Gillian: of all the things he wanted to do to her, all the things he wanted her to do to him, all the things they'd do to each other. Finally giving up on the idea of getting any rest, he'd tried to work on his genetic mapping model.

In the past, whenever aspects of his life became unpleasant—even during those seemingly unending days when his body had screamed with pain and he'd distracted himself by running equations in his mind—he'd been able to lose himself in his research. And if crunching numbers didn't prove to be the answer, he'd then take off to some new war zone and spend weeks or months compiling complex personality profiles and DNA samples from the population that he could plug into his behavioral prediction equations.

The distraction of work had never failed him. Until now. Until he'd made the major mistake of bringing Gillian Cassidy into his life. Further irritating were two more phone calls—one from Van Horn, another from the Pentagon, checking on his progress.

While he found them both irksome, Hunter was becoming most annoyed with the military brass. Accustomed to looking at things in black and white, and action-oriented, they couldn't seem to understand that some things took time. He also understood that, given the opportunity, they'd be as eager as the Russians to use his research for less-than-altruistic ends.

"Calls like this are a distraction," he told the general who headed up the military committee for his project. "I can't get any work done if I'm always talking on the damn phone."

The conversation was short, brief and, as always when dealing with this particular branch of government, unsatisfying. Still, just before he hung up, Hunter assured the general, who was also in charge of writing out the checks, that he expected a breakthrough soon.

Even knowing that he should rerun the numbers, Hunter found himself riveted in his chair, his eyes glued to the monitor, watching Gillian sleep alone in his wide bed.

From the way she'd tossed and turned, from the soft little sounds she'd made and the way her hands had unconsciously stroked her body like a lover's caress, it was clear that he was not the only one burning up from the inside out. Unfortunately, that thought didn't offer a great deal of comfort.

She was supposed to burn, dammit. While his mind was supposed to remain cool and analytical.

She'd disappeared into the bathroom. Hunter waited impatiently, rewarded a few minutes later when she returned engulfed in his oversize robe. It surrounded her, embraced her in a way that stimulated a new carnal image of slowly unwrapping her from those thick folds of terry cloth. Although the idea of watching her in the shower had proved more than a little appealing, in the end, he'd reluctantly left the camera out of the bathroom.

Now, looking at the triangle of pale skin framed by the vee of the robe's lapels, contrasting so vividly with the black material, Hunter found himself wishing that he hadn't allowed himself that chivalrous impulse.

A drop of moisture sparkled like a diamond displayed on white satin; Hunter groaned, struck with a harsh, visceral need to lick it off.

He reached for the remote control, determined to turn the damn thing off, to darken the screen and return to work. But he couldn't do it.

Obsession. The word, which heretofore he'd only allowed to be applied to his work, tolled in his head like the deep, lonely sound of the foghorns that echoed in the mists outside his house.

Hunter had never been a man given to deep introspection, he'd always saved complex analysis for his research. But he didn't have to be a genius to realize that somehow, when he hadn't been looking, he'd developed an unhealthy preoccupation with his old nemesis' lovely daughter.

He'd have to send her away. Soon.

That decided, and knowing that the decent, honorable thing to do would be to allow her some small privacy while she dressed, Hunter reluctantly darkened the screen.

But instead of returning to work, he remained in the leather chair as his rebellious mind created wildly erotic mental pictures that made the Kama Sutra seem tame by comparison.

GILLIAN FOLLOWED the enticing scent of coffee to the kitchen, where she found Mildred Adams at the counter, chopping vegetables for tonight's dinner. Unlike the cold sterility of Hunter's hedonistic bedroom, the kitchen was warmly domestic, with copper kettles and gleaming marble countertops.

It also offered what she suspected would be a breathtaking view of the ocean. Unfortunately today the sea was draped in a misty veil of fog.

"Good morning." Gillian greeted the housekeeper with a faint, embarrassed smile. "I can't believe I slept so late." She hated the idea of Mrs. Adams believing she was typically so slothful. It was bad enough to have the housekeeper think she was sleeping with Hunter.

The older woman shrugged. "Dr. St. John said you'd be tired." She began attacking a carrot, slicing it into neat little circles with amazing speed. "You had a busy day yesterday."

"Yes," Gillian murmured. "It was that."

"He also said you've been traveling around the world, playing piano concerts." She stopped her work and poured a cup of coffee into a thick blue spatterware mug.

"I returned to the States last week."

The cup was warm in her hands. Lured by the enticing steam rising from the dark depths, Gillian took a tentative sip.

"Oh, this is delicious." She sighed her pleasure and took another, longer drink.

"Hope it's not too strong for you. I made it the way Dr. St. John likes it."

"It's perfect."

"Dr. St. John says coffee should be as hot as hell-fire, thick as marsh mud, and as black as a witch's heart." Mildred swept the carrots aside and wiped her hands on her apron. "You'll be wanting breakfast."

"Oh, it's already so late. I don't want to bother you."

"It's my job," Mildred reminded her briskly as she opened the oversize refrigerator.

Thirty minutes later, after an enormous meal of corned beef hash topped with a poached egg and potato-flour muffins spread with homemade blueberry conserve, Gillian didn't think she'd ever be able to move again.

She'd never been much of a breakfast eater, but uncomfortable about what Mildred Adams knew—or suspected—about her reason for being here, she hadn't wanted to make waves.

"I believe I'll take a walk," she decided.

"That's a good idea. Dr. St. John bought you some winter outdoor wear. It'll be hanging by the back door in the mudroom."

"Dr. St. John seems to have thought of everything."

Gillian's dry tone seemed to fly over the woman's head. "He figured, bein' a Californian, you wouldn't have the proper clothing for our Maine winter. You'd best bundle up real good, since it's blowing like old Gabe's horn out there.

"Oh, and the piano got delivered this morning," Mildred said on an apparent afterthought as Gillian started to leave the kitchen.

That stopped her in her tracks. "The piano?"

"The one Dr. St. John ordered. It was scheduled to be here two days ago, but the driver blew a tire in Augusta and got held up. Dr. St. John t'weren't at all pleased about that," she tacked on with a dark frown.

"I'll just bet he wasn't."

Having witnessed firsthand Hunter's seeming need to control every aspect of his environment, Gillian could just picture his irritation at his instructions not being carried out to the letter.

"Does he play?" Too late, Gillian remembered the hook that had replaced Hunter's left hand.

"Not that I know of." Mildred finished putting Gillian's dishes in the dishwasher and added detergent. "He said you might enjoy having it here."

Dammit! Just when she thought she was getting a handle on the man, he did something generous. "He's right."

Along with her lingering concern for her father, who hadn't been looking all that well when she'd answered his frantic summons in Cambridge, the other thing that had bothered Gillian most about this trip was the prospect of going thirty long days without her music.

"They put it in the library," Mildred said as she began attacking a stewing chicken with a cleaver. "Third door on the left down the hall. The man guaranteed me that he'd tuned it properly, but Dr. St. John said that if you don't find it satisfactory, I'm to call and make him come back and do it right.''

With that flat, no-nonsense Yankee voice, and the vicious cleaver in her hand, Mildred Adams definitely looked like someone to be reckoned with. Gillian had not a single doubt that the piano tuner would have done his best to avoid this crusty woman's displeasure.

''I'm sure it'll be fine.''

Gillian still intended to take a walk to try to burn off some of the extensive calories she'd just consumed, but her curiosity had her heading toward the library.

Hunter's unrelenting concern for detail was evident in everything about the vast room that smelled like leather and lemon oil. The soaring cathedral ceiling glowed with the radiance of western red cedar, adding a soothing warmth that contrasted with the gray sky outside the glass wall.

A fire crackled in a stone fireplace large enough to stand in. Bookcases lined three walls, and although there were the leather-bound classics one might expect to find in such an impressive room, the bright dust jackets and paperback editions also crowding the shelves gave proof that the library had been designed for use, not merely show.

The furniture was ox-blood leather and oversize, inviting visitors to settle in and burrow down with a good book.

Claiming the center of the floor was a gleaming, nine-foot black Steinway piano, a twin of the model she'd bought with the royalties when her first CD went platinum.

At the time she'd justified the cost, and her uncharacteristically self-indulgent behavior, by reminding herself that the piano's unsurpassed tone—with its soft treble and deep bass—could only improve her music.

But for Hunter to have spent so much money for the short amount of time she was going to be staying here on Castle Mountain was astonishing. If he was actually expecting her to pay off such a glorious instrument with sexual services in a mere month's time, they could both be in trouble.

Gillian recalled the long-ago holiday when she'd put on her best ivory angora sweater and matching wool skirt and the pair of pearl earrings her father had given her for Christmas, then arranged to be sitting at the piano in the music room adjacent to the foyer when Hunter arrived at her parents' house.

While the maid took his coat, she'd launched into a rendition of Chopin's Fantaisie Impromptu in C-sharp Minor, which she found wondrously romantic and had been laboring over for weeks. Just for him. This would be the night he finally noticed her. Tonight he would hear the love she felt for him in her music and finally realize that they were soul mates!

Unfortunately, all those hours of practice had gone in vain as her mother called out his name in a voice that sounded like silver bells, causing him to walk past the open doorway without so much as a sideways glance inside.

The memory made her sigh. Then, drawn to the

gleaming ebony and ivory keys, she played an arpeggio and was pleased but not overly surprised to find the tuning perfect. She ran through a few bars of George Winston's "Colors" and found the response of the keys to her touch sublime.

Tempted to play longer, Gillian knew from experience that were she to sit down, she'd lose track of the time and the next thing she knew it would be evening and time for her next encounter with the man who insisted on becoming more than just her lover. She might not be experienced, but she understood, all too well, that Hunter viewed himself as her would-be sexual master.

Whenever she considered the idea intellectually, the successful, talented woman dwelling inside Gillian found it appalling. Or ridiculous, like that silly television sitcom she watched occasionally on late-night cable, the one about the astronaut and the girl he kept in a bottle.

Yet at the same time, Hunter had always been, to her, a siren call. It was admittedly politically incorrect, nevertheless, since she'd arrived here last evening, she was amazed to discover the idea of surrendering control to such a ruthless, demanding man, opening herself up to all the eroticism she knew he would bring to their encounter, unreasonably alluring.

While she'd dressed this morning, forced to forego underwear, she'd almost managed to convince herself that such an exploration of the erotic side of love would be good for her art. Her music had always reflected her own innermost feelings, fantasies and dreams. That being the case, wouldn't this sensual knowledge allow her to play with more depth? More passion?

"Who do you think you're kidding?"

She attacked the keyboard, pounding out a series of hard, angry percussive bass chords that echoed off the walls and ceiling.

"This isn't about art." She heaped an extra helping of sarcasm on the word. "It's about lust. Pure and simple. You want him, dammit."

Her short, bitter laugh was directed at herself. "You just don't want him to know how badly. And you're also too used to being the one calling all the shots to surrender control to anyone."

While she certainly hadn't reached Hunter's level of success, Gillian wasn't intimidated by either his fame or his brilliance. What did worry her was that although she was willing to surrender her body, she feared Hunter would not be satisfied until he took possession of her heart. And worse yet, her soul.

Sighing, she turned away from the piano and left the library. A walk in the brisk Maine sea air would do her good.

"It'll clear your head," she said, giving herself a little pep talk as she found the Christmas-red parka Mildred had told her about hanging on a hook in the mudroom. It would also help her decide exactly how she was going to handle Hunter when he returned with new demands tonight.

SHE LIKED IT. He'd hoped she would. Hunter watched, foolishly, ridiculously pleased, as Gillian stroked the ebony surface of the piano, ran her long, slender fingers over the keys in soaring legato runs, smiling in response to the exquisite sound. It was such a simple thing, really.

The Steinway, as expensive as it was, didn't come close to the price of the Ferrari parked alongside the Suburban and the Mercedes in the three-car garage. But it obviously possessed a value beyond price to Gillian, and seeing her eyes light up as she played a brief passage from some New Age piece he recognized but could not name, he realized that she would have been no more delighted if he'd suddenly entered the library from the secret panel in the wall and dumped the glittering Hope diamond into her hand.

As he had the first time he'd seen her on tape, playing her beloved piano at Stonehenge, he marveled over the soft, lit-from-within hue of her eyes, the delicate bone structure of her face, the lush shape of her mouth.

He shifted in the chair, having to adjust the jeans that had suddenly become too tight as he remembered, with vivid accuracy, exactly how luscious her silky breasts had felt in his hands. He wanted her. More than ever. And, from her muttered reference to lust, he knew that although she might refuse to admit it to him just yet, she wanted him, too. Which should have made things simple.

But as he watched her stroke the gleaming wood, Hunter was stuck by the unwelcome realization that even stronger than the physical need that had him tied up in knots, was his desire to have Gillian smile at him the way she'd smiled at that damn piano.

THE FOG HAD NEARLY LIFTED. All that remained were little wisps of mist that twined around Gillian's ankles as she walked along the edge of the rocky granite cliff. The anvil sky still hung low over the water, although every so often, there'd be a part in the clouds, like a slit in a heavy gray velvet theater curtain, inviting a shaft of stuttering sunshine to peek through.

Although Hunter's foresight in supplying her with winter clothing irked, she was decidedly grateful for the hooded parka and insulated hiking boots. What passed for a winter jacket in California—even in relatively chilly Monterey—would be a joke here in Maine. Ice crystals sparkled in an air so brisk and cold it literally took her breath away as it cleared her head. Comfortably cocooned in the thick down jacket, she stayed surprisingly and pleasantly warm.

The site atop the jagged blue-gray cliff where Hunter had chosen to build his house was dazzling. It also reminded her a great deal of her own home, which she'd been renting for the past two years. She'd attempted to purchase the small seaside cottage, but the owner, a cardiologist in San Francisco, had proven distressingly sentimental, refusing to give up the modest little clapboard cottage with its million-dollar view that had originally belonged to his grandmother.

In the distance, a tall-masted fishing boat chugged through the silver capped waves, then disappeared over the horizon. Below her, down on the beach, a trio of men, clad in high black boots and bright sunshine-yellow slickers walked behind the retreating tide, using rakes in the wet gray sand to uncover the clams, which were, in this part of the world, as valuable as a pirate's booty.

Seagulls followed in their wake, noisily demanding a handout, while other, more self-sufficient birds dove into the receding waters, emerging with shells in their beaks, which they dropped onto the sand to open.

Unfortunately, more often than not, scavenger gulls were first to arrive at the broken shell, stealing the fleshy innards out from under the beak of the bird who'd worked for his meal. The small drama was familiar; she'd witnessed it innumerable times on her own coast.

Gillian had been uneasy, almost disoriented since her arrival on Castle Mountain. Now, as she walked along the cliff, marveling at the beauty of earth, stone, sky and water, laughing at the antics of the greedy gulls, she felt herself beginning to relax.

She was on her way back to the house when a sound caught her attention. Searching for the source of the strange mewling, she looked up into the branches of a hardy scrub pine clinging tenaciously to the very edge of the cliff and spotted a ball of multicolored fur.

"Well, hello." Her words came out on little ghost-like puffs of icy breath. "What are you doing up there?"

The animal's response was an arched back and an unwelcoming hiss.

Not wanting to frighten it, she stood where she was and put her hands deep into the pockets of her parka. The cat's long fur was a striped mixture of black, orange and cream. It had a white ruff around its neck, long pointed ears and bright greenish-gold eyes that looked as though they'd been rimmed with kohl, giving it a masked appearance. A tail thickened as it swished back and forth, warning her to keep her distance.

"You look hungry," she said gently. More than hungry. Beneath that filthy, matted fur, the cat appeared distressingly scrawny. "When was the last time you had a decent meal?"

The cat responded with another angry hiss.

"If I'd known I was going to run into you, I would have brought some food from the house. There was certainly enough of it." She thought back on the biscuits she'd eaten. "If you want to wait right here, I could go back and—"

Without warning, the cat sprang from the tree, deftly landed on all fours, then took off running into a bank of fog.

"I guess not," Gillian murmured, knowing it would be folly to try to catch it.

But as she continued walking back to the house, she couldn't get the half-starved creature from her mind.

7

HUNTER STOOD AT THE WALL of glass that looked out over the sea and watched Gillian walking along the cliff. The day had dawned gray and cold; in the scarlet parka, she reminded him of a brilliant cardinal. He was also surprised, once again, at how small she was, how delicate-looking.

He saw her stop at a tree not far from the front drive, watched as she slipped her hands into her pockets and seemed to be talking up at it. A moment later a coon cat bailed from the limb. He watched her watching it and realized he was beginning to be able to read her mind.

"It won't do you any good," he murmured five minutes later, when she returned to the tree with a plastic bag of food she scattered on the ground around the trunk. "You may as well try to tame a tiger."

Although he knew there was no way she could hear him through the wall of glass, Hunter was surprised when Gillian suddenly glanced up and looked straight at him.

For a suspended moment their gazes met, then held. Then she did something totally unexpected.

She smiled.

And every muscle in his stomach constricted.

His gut wasn't the only thing affected. Hunter slid a look downward and cursed. His mutinous body, ever ready, had leaped to response.

Yet more proof that George Cassidy had been right about one thing—emotions definitely clouded logic. For six months after being forced from MIT, wallowing in self-pity, Hunter had drunk himself into oblivion. He'd been on a steep slope straight into alcohol hell when he'd caught a glimpse of a seedy-looking boozer in the convex security mirror in a Cambridge liquor store. That he was looking at himself hadn't immediately sunk in. When it did, he'd walked out of the store, leaving the bottle of high-octane comfort he'd paid for on the counter.

He'd gone back to his apartment, showered, shaved and, using the scissors that came with his Swiss Army knife, had hacked away at his long, stringy hair, giving himself his first haircut in months.

Unsurprising, the only thing in his refrigerator had been three bottles of beer and something green and furry he'd vaguely remembered being a brick of sharp cheddar cheese. Hungry for the first time in a very long while, he'd uncovered the phone beneath a pile of dirty laundry and ordered a pizza. And a six-pack of Pepsi.

While wolfing down the pizza, he'd pulled out a yellow legal pad and had begun a harsh, unrelenting review of his life.

Looking at things rationally, he'd finally admitted to not being surprised by his mentor's betrayal. Everyone knew that the seemingly placid ivy-covered halls of academia were nothing more than a facade, effectively concealing what could only be described as a shark tank.

If you didn't keep swimming forward, you died. Pure and simple. And Cassidy, as king of the sharks, had no intention of dying anytime soon. Which was why he'd chosen to eat Hunter instead.

Deciding that his former mentor was right, that emotions were a liability in this scientific world of sharks and cannibalistic bunnies, Hunter had set about putting his often volatile feelings into cold storage. Where they'd remained out of sight, and comfortably out of mind, until he'd made the fatal mistake of bringing Gillian Cassidy to Castle Mountain.

It was as if she'd arrived with her own personal blowtorch, determined to melt the ice that had dwelt within him for so long.

And that, Hunter vowed grimly as he turned away from the window, was something he could not allow.

THIS WAS GETTING ridiculous, Gillian decided on her fourth night on Castle Mountain. She was sitting in the kitchen, as she did every night—alone—eating her solitary supper. Hunter had made his purpose plain from the beginning, on her first night in the house when he'd kissed her senseless and stimulated feelings she'd never even known existed inside her.

Feelings that continued to boil like one of Mildred Adams's rich and hearty stews. When she reached for a crusty piece of bread, her nipples brushed against her sweater in a way that was anything but comforting. That was another thing that was driving her crazy.

She'd always found cashmere to be the softest of wools. And, perhaps it was. But these past days, forced to go without underwear, she was all too aware of the fibers brushing continually against her nipples, bringing them to a state of near constant arousal.

She'd given up wearing her warm but scratchy tweed slacks the second day. Unfortunately, that left her with a pair of jeans that cut into her crotch, stimulating her sensitive clitoris to a point just this side of pain, or her long, fluid skirts that when worn without panties left her feeling unnervingly vulnerable.

Which was, she suspected, exactly the way Hunter wanted her.

So, here she was, her mind having accepted her seduction, her body aching for him to just get it over with, and what had Hunter done? Locked himself away in his damn laboratory, or lair, or whatever the hell he called it, leaving her to think about him, to dream about him in ways that did nothing to comfort.

Even without the constant thoughts of sex, the simple truth was that she was just plain lonely. Mrs. Adams might be a great cook, but she was a typically taciturn New Englander.

Besides, even if she was willing to chat, she wasn't a woman Gillian would be comfortable sharing her thoughts with. Especially the ones she'd been having lately, Gillian thought as she recalled, with vivid clarity, last night's all-too-stimulating dream where she'd been a lusty Celtic peasant girl. Of course, Hunter had played the role of an invading Norman, who'd taken the concept of rape and plunder to amazing extremes.

The all-too-vivid memory of the many sexual

things he'd done to her, the brazen things she'd encouraged, then ultimately begged him to do, made Gillian blush even now. They also made her ache.

"It's part of his intimidation tactics," she told herself as she slathered the bread with creamy butter and took a huge bite. The crusty bread was thick and yeasty, the melted butter smooth as warm silk against her tongue. "He's playing hard to get, waiting for you to surrender your pride.

"Well, it isn't going to work." She glared down at the robust stew and jabbed a piece of lamb. "I'm not going to play his damn game any longer."

In fact, she decided as she chewed furiously, part of the problem had been that Hunter had set the agenda from the beginning. It was time, she decided, for her to make a move.

Picking up her plate and the glass of wine, she left the kitchen and headed off to confront the dragon in his den.

ALTHOUGH IT HADN'T BEEN easy ignoring the lure of the hidden video screens tracking Gillian's moves, Hunter had actually begun to get some work done. When he heard the determined footfalls marching toward him down the hall, he sighed and decided that the woman might look like spun sugar, but she definitely had a steel core. He should have realized Gillian wouldn't continue to play by his rules forever.

She entered the room without even bothering to knock.

"This Beauty and the Beast scenario is getting boring," she announced.

He saved his data, darkened the screen, then turned from the computer. "Beauty and the Beast?"

"Every morning Mrs. Adams has my breakfast waiting for me when I get up. Dinner, as you colorful islanders call it, is served promptly at noon, and every night, at six on the dot, my supper appears on the dining room table, where I'm expected to eat it, again, alone. It's beginning to remind me of all those invisible servants feeding Beauty."

"I suppose the analogy is somewhat valid," he allowed, thinking that she certainly fit the title role. "Because you're stunningly beautiful."

In her flowing scarlet skirt that skimmed the tops of her boots and matching tunic-length cashmere cardigan sweater she reminded him of a small, defiant flame. He rubbed his chin and realized that once again he'd forgotten to shave.

"I am curious, though. Do you see me as a beast?"

Hunter knew that despite his obvious physical scars, some women, prone to flattering a man, would hasten to assure him they thought nothing of the kind. He was pleased when once again Gillian demonstrated that she was a breed apart.

"I don't know." She sat down on the leather couch, pushed aside some papers and put her bowl on the low granite table in front of her. "You're certainly far from civilized. But a beast?"

She gave him a long, judicious look, earning more points when he couldn't detect any overt pity in her moss-green eyes. "I suppose I'll have to think about that."

"Why don't you do that," he agreed.

She glanced around the office that Hunter knew was an anachronism, a definite throwback to another time with its dark woods, shelves of leather-bound books and antique sailing paraphernalia. Although he'd never really had any roots to speak of, the first time he'd stepped foot on Castle Mountain he'd felt as if he'd come home.

He'd spent his rare free time the past three years on the phone to antique dealers up and down the Maine coast, collecting a half-dozen framed schooner prints, a trio of whaling harpoons, a brass ship lantern and the ridiculously expensive group of scrimshaw figures.

"I'm a bit disappointed," she said.

Hunter arched a brow, inviting elaboration.

"Well, as intriguing as this room admittedly is, it certainly doesn't look like a mad scientist's lair." She shook her head and picked up a small ivory carving of a whale. "No steaming, bubbling sulfurous beakers, no petri dishes growing green alien life-forms, no mold-covered, wet stone walls that could have come from some Transylvanian castle."

She exchanged the whale for a miniature pewter schooner. "The least you could do is have a few bodies laid out on slabs with electrodes attached to their shaved heads."

"If I'd known you expected Dr. Frankenstein's laboratory, I would have arranged to have some rats scurrying around in dark corners."

"Rats aren't necessary." She shivered visibly at the thought. "Actually, this is quite cozy."

"I'm pleased you approve."

The hell of it was that Hunter really was pleased. He shouldn't care whether or not Gillian liked anything about his house. After all, in less than thirty days she'd be leaving. Back to her own life in California.

"I definitely do." She picked up her spoon and pointed at the bowl on the desk. "Your stew's going to get cold. Why don't you bring it over here and we can eat together like normal people living together under the same roof."

"So, you consider our situation normal?"

"Of course I do… Why, I'm always being brought to isolated locations as some man's sex slave….

"The first time was when I was dragged into a taxi after a glorious day in the Louvre by an eccentric Parisian painter who used to paint Monet's *Water Lilies* all over me with flavored syrups, then lick them off."

"There's a thought," Hunter murmured, idly wondering if Mrs. Adams kept any Hershey's syrup in the pantry.

"Oh, he was a nice-enough man, despite being a kidnapper, but the chocolate kept clogging my pores and made my skin break out terribly, so at first I wasn't at all unhappy when he sold me to a Swiss banker who lived in a nine-hundred-year-old house built like a cuckoo clock, dressed me in dirndls like Heidi and yodeled every time he came."

She shook her head with mock regret. "Unfortunately, he tasted like sausage and beer, so you can imagine how relieved I was when he passed me on to one of his bank's clients, a Saudi sheikh who flew me back to his country himself, in his luxurious jet.''

Her eyes turned reminiscent, her lips curved in a slow smile as she took a drink of the ruby-red cabernet sauvignon.

''When we landed in his country, his servants were waiting with a pair of the most beautiful Arabian stallions I'd ever seen. It was dark when we arrived, but unlike tonight, there was a full moon that floated like a ghostly galleon in the sky. We rode a long way out into the desert, our way guided by that huge silver moon to a tent beneath the stars that had been erected just for us.''

Hunter understood that she'd begun the tale as a joke, to sensually taunt him with her erotic stories as he'd been taunting her with his absence.

Interestingly, the tables had seemed to turn. Looking at her flushed cheeks and overly bright eyes, he realized that she was becoming aroused by her own words. She'd never looked more beautiful. Or more desirable.

He took the glass from her hand, slowly turning it so that the faint pink crescent left by her lips was facing him.

''Don't stop now. It's just getting interesting.''

She seemed enthralled as he took a drink from that same place her lips had touched. More color touched her cheeks, her throat. He half expected her to stop, but was ridiculously pleased when she continued.

''We'd no sooner arrived when a pair of gorgeous, incredibly handsome nearly nude servants undressed me, then bathed me, inside and out, in scented water upon which they'd scattered orchid petals.''

Once again it crossed Hunter's mind that she was an excellent actress. Her husky voice vibrated with sex and sin.

''While the guy lounged back on velvet pillows and watched,'' Hunter guessed.

Gillian shrugged. ''Since I was, at least for the time being, his property, it was Khamil's show. That was his name. Prince Khamil.'' She closed her eyes, leaned her head against the back of the couch and sighed. ''To be perfectly honest, the experience was sublime.''

Her words excited him, as he knew she'd intended.

Hunter had spent the past four days staying away from her, determined to test his control to the limit. He'd waited long enough, he decided on a burst of resolve as he returned his attention to her erotic tale.

''It was amazing,'' she was saying. A milky topaz ring gleamed like the ghostly moon she'd described as she combed her hand through her long hair. Her voice had taken on a rich, breathless quality that had Hunter biting back a groan.

''After I was bathed, the servants rubbed fragrant oil over every inch of my body, preparing me for their master's ravishments. Then, when I was gleaming like molten gold and feeling every bit as hot and danger-ous, he dismissed them.

''At that moment, we could have been the only two people in the world. In the universe.''

Just like tonight, Hunter thought as her gaze drifted out the wall of glass into the huge dark void outside.

He wondered if she was realizing that they were every bit as isolated as she and her fictional Arab prince.

"And what happened then?" he asked, his voice roughened from a desire too long denied.

Gillian turned away from the ebony night sky. As her gaze collided with Hunter's, he could tell that she realized the waiting was coming to an end.

She shrugged again, seeming to tire of the game. "I forget."

"It's just as well. I've never thought of myself as a jealous man, but with you I just might make an exception. Having to listen to the nitty-gritty details of your erotic adventures might just make me want to go kill your depraved desert sheikh."

"He was fictional, Hunter," she said softly, as if concerned he hadn't understood her stories had been merely a game.

"I realize that. Which is why I'm finding the impulse to murder even more puzzling."

He took another sip of her wine. "You are, by the way, a very good storyteller. I could easily imagine myself listening to Scheherazade weave her entertaining tales."

"But Scheherazade had to come up with a thousand stories. My time here is going to be much briefer."

"True." For some reason, although he'd been telling himself that he was going to have to send her away before the deadline he himself had imposed, Hunter found that idea less than appealing.

Needing something stronger than the excellent cabernet sauvignon he'd had delivered by Ben Adams's mail packet from the mainland, he stood up, crossed the room to the antique sea captain's chest where he kept the liquor and poured a splash of cognac into a glass.

A strange aura settled over the room. A tense mood that was definitely not conducive to romance.

No, not romance, Hunter reminded himself as he swallowed the liquor. Sex. That's all it was. That's all he would allow it to be.

He watched her take another bite of stew. Watched her swallow and resisted touching his mouth to her smooth white throat.

"You must be working on something important," she said, glancing over at the computer. It was more than a little obvious that she was eager to change the subject. And the mood. Which, of course, was impossible now.

"You could say that," he answered obliquely, not wanting to get into the details of his multimillion dollar grant from the government.

Hunter knew, all too well, that the project could prove to be personally dangerous. Even today the general had warned him of rumors of yet another terrorist group who'd put a bounty on his life. As if he needed a reminder after the letter-bomb attack in Bosnia. With a pragmatic eye to the future, he considered the sacrifice of a hand a small price to pay for the chance to contribute to world peace.

"I suppose you're like my father. Oh, I wasn't accusing you of plagiarism, Hunter," she said quickly when he immediately scowled at that less-than-flattering comparison.

"I meant that when you're deep in a project, you probably lose track of the world around you. Food, for instance." She pointed out his still untouched stew. "Time. Perhaps even days."

Ah. Comprehension dawned. She was wondering why he'd been ignoring her. Hunter wondered with a twisted humor that was directed inward what she'd say if he told her that he'd been wondering the same thing himself.

"I suppose I could be accused of being the stereotypical absentminded scientist from time to time." He sat down at his desk again and stabbed a piece of potato.

"I was hoping for an opportunity to thank you for the piano."

"You don't have to thank me. I've been enjoying the free concerts."

"You can hear me?" Her eyes widened. "I'm sorry. The house is so large, I'd thought for sure that my music wouldn't have disturbed your work."

She dragged her hand through her hair again in a nervous gesture he'd come to recognize. "I remember how my father hated any distractions. I never would have played so much if I'd known."

"Don't worry about it." He waved her apology away with his fork, damning himself for having made such a stupid mistake. If she had any idea that he'd installed cameras and microphones throughout the house...

"As I said, I enjoy hearing you play. You're very good."

She managed a soft smile, but the concern didn't

leave her eyes. "It would be hard not to sound good on that piano. It's an incredible instrument. And awfully extravagant."

"I can afford it."

"It was still a very nice thing for you to do."

"Trust me, Gillian, I'm never nice. The piano was simply a means to an end. If you're relaxed and happy during the day, it stands to reason you'll be more relaxed at night."

He took another bite of stew, wondering why it was that he'd never noticed what an exceptionally good cook his housekeeper was.

"Mrs. Adams tells me you've taking up trapping."

"Trapping?" She glanced up at him uncomprehendingly. "Oh, the cat." Her grin was quick and all too appealing. "The poor thing was starving. I just thought he could use a little food."

The smile faded from her face, as if she'd just realized that perhaps the food hadn't been hers to give. "I hope you don't mind—"

"Of course not."

What kind of man did she think he was, that he'd refuse a few bites of roast or chicken for an abandoned animal?

"I just think I should warn you not to get your hopes up. That's a Maine coon cat, Gillian. And although the breed's become popular among cat fanciers, that one's feral. You're not going to turn him into a soft, playful house tabby by feeding him Mrs. Adams's chicken breasts."

"A coon cat? Are you saying he's part raccoon?"

"Folklore says they are. But they're actually just

called that because they look so much like raccoons. History has it that they were brought to Maine by European traders and sailors who used them as rat catchers on their ships. They were domesticated as farm cats, but many escaped to roam in the wild. That's obviously what's happened with yours.''

"He was afraid of me in the beginning,'' she divulged. "But I think we're beginning to understand each other. Because today he nearly took a piece of sausage out of my hand.''

"It's just as well he didn't. He'd probably take your finger off. And there's always a chance he's rabid.''

"Oh, I'm sure he's not,'' she said quickly. So quickly Hunter knew her impetuous words came from her heart rather than her head. "I'm hoping to get him to trust me enough to let me get him to a vet.''

He laughed at that, a rough bark that sounded rusty even to his own ears. "You'd have to stay here for a thousand days for that to happen. He's wild, Gillian. Wild and fiercely independent. Even your soft feminine heart won't be able to tame him.''

She lifted her chin; her moss-green eyes gleamed with a challenge he found all too enticing.

"Well, we'll just have to see about that, won't we?''

She returned to her stew.

They ate in silence. And Hunter, who never allowed anyone into his office, was surprised at how comfortable it felt.

8

"WOULD YOU DO SOMETHING for me?"

Hunter's sudden question, asked in a quiet, even voice caused Gillian to lift her head. His eyes were smooth and cool. She wondered if it was only her overly active imagination that had her sensing a faint discomfiture in them.

"I didn't think I had a choice." She met his impenetrable gaze straight on.

"You've always had a choice, Gillian."

"Oh?" Even knowing that arguing with a man who held so much of her future—and her father's—in his hands could be considered folly, Gillian arched a brow. "You wouldn't let me leave that first night," she reminded him.

"If you truly believe that I would have honestly made you to remain here against your will, you're not the woman I thought you were."

He shook his head with obviously mock chagrin. "Perhaps it's time to send you back to your father. Where you'll be safe."

His proposal was tinged with an acid sarcasm that suggested he didn't believe her father had had her safety in mind when he'd persuaded her to come to

Castle Mountain in the first place. And, dammit, Gillian acknowledged reluctantly, he was right.

The sad truth was that George Cassidy's own needs would always be of primary interest to him. If she were to be brutally honest with herself, she'd have to admit that she probably ranked somewhere below a cage of white laboratory rats in her father's hierarchy.

Part of the problem, of course, was that she'd never done anything to truly compel his attention her way. In an attempt to avoid making waves, she'd always tried to be the quiet, dutiful daughter. Seen but not heard, admired on those special occasions when he'd use her as an example of his superior genes, putting her on display like a champion King Charles spaniel at a Westminster dog show, only to be forgotten the rest of the time.

Perhaps she should have rocked the boat more, Gillian considered belatedly. Caused a few more problems, or even embarrassed him publicly. Of course, he'd undoubtedly have been furious if she'd started showing up in after-hour clubs with green hair and pierced body parts, but at least anger was a strong, deeply felt human emotion. It would have been better than nothing.

Hunter watched the range of feeling wash across Gillian's face: irritation, frustration, pain, regret, and then something that looked a great deal like humor, even though he personally couldn't find anything amusing about her situation.

"Something funny?"

"I was just wondering what my father would have

done if I'd shown up at his lab with a silver ring in one eyebrow.''

Hunter shrugged. "What makes you think he'd notice?''

Good point. "Are you always this cruel?''

"No. I am, however, always this truthful. There may be times you might not like what I say, Gillian, because sometimes the truth hurts. But I'll never lie to you.''

"Though you might hurt me.''

"I told you, I'd never do—''

"Anything I don't want you to do," she broke in.

"That's right.''

She didn't immediately say anything.

As scintillating scenes of what she'd dreamed of him doing to her, with her, spun in her mind like the tumbling, glittery facets of a kaleidoscope, Gillian couldn't say anything. She took another sip meant to soothe and realized her mistake when the wine only made her blood warmer. The tension rose, stringing between them like the silken cords of a deadly spider's web.

A web where Hunter sat in the center, watching.

Waiting.

Her lips were dry. Too dry. Forgoing the wine this time, she licked them, realizing her mistake when she caught the spark of hot hunger in Hunter's formerly too cool eyes.

"What exactly is it you want me to do?" It was barely a whisper, but easily heard in the cathedral-like stillness of the room. Gillian braced herself for the worst.

"I thought it might be nice if you'd play for me."

"Play?" Her eyes widened. "The piano?"

"Do you have a problem performing for an audience of one?"

"No. It's just that I..."

She lowered her eyes, and in trying to escape Hunter's steady gaze, Gillian found herself staring at that huge bulge beneath the denim jeans.

She'd done that, she realized with a sense of feminine awe. She'd made his body hard, had caused his eyes to darken with lust. She was the source of the male hunger radiating from him, making her more aware of her own body than ever before in her life.

She was also more nervous than she'd ever been in her life. Including that memorable time when she'd first played in public. Utilizing a relaxing technique she employed before going on stage in her concerts, she willed her mind to calm and pictured a peaceful tropical lagoon. The sand, beneath the shimmering rays of a soothing sun, glistened as if diamonds had been spilled from a pirate's treasure chest onto the shore; the water was a deep jade green and was lapping ever so gently against the sand while winds whispered in the fronds of the palm trees overhead. Nearby, a liquid silver waterfall tumbled over a lush green cliff.

The image, taught to her by a psychotherapist to rid her of stage fright early in her career, never failed to work. It was again tonight until suddenly, without warning, a man appeared from behind that frothy, falling water. He was tall and dark and fully aroused, resembling an ancient fertility god carved from a mahogany tree trunk.

As he began moving toward her, in a loose-hipped predatory stride, Gillian realized he was not some inanimate god carved from wood, but a man. A man who wanted her. A man who was unnervingly, unmistakably familiar.

"That was fascinating."

Hunter's low voice reverberated like the growl of a jungle beast, making it momentarily difficult for Gillian to separate fantasy from reality. Gingerly lifting her gaze, she viewed the unbanked lust in his eyes.

"I was watching your face," he said. "You were on the verge of orgasm, all by yourself."

"I was not." Gillian was unnerved by the way he'd read her private thoughts so easily. "And you're wrong."

"Want to put it to the test, sweetheart?" He did not use the word as an endearment, but a dare. "I'll bet it'd only take one touch to send you over the edge."

He spread his fingers on his thigh, enticing her attention back to his erection. The sight of that hardness, mingled with the lingering image of her waterfall fantasy, caused a deep yearning to touch. To be touched. All over.

"I thought you wanted me to play for you."

"I told you, Gillian, I want everything. But I believe, in civilized circles, that seduction is best begun with good food and wine, which we've already had. Then music is a nice next step."

''As you've already pointed out, Hunter, I accepted your terms by coming to Castle Mountain. Seduction isn't necessary.''

He didn't answer immediately. Just gave her another of those long looks that Gillian found impossible to read.

''Actually,'' he stated finally, just as her nerves had reached their screeching point, ''it is.'' He stood up and held out his hand to her.

And as they walked, fingers linked—almost like friends, or lovers—from the room, Hunter wondered what Gillian would say if she knew that she was the first woman he'd ever felt the need to take the time to seduce.

In the beginning, it was Gillian who should have fled.

Now, as they entered the library, Hunter decided that if he had any instincts for self-preservation left, this would be the time for him to take off running.

A fire had been laid earlier in the evening. Outside the wall of glass, sea and sky melded together like an ebony satin comforter. Gillian stood in the doorway, watching as Hunter casually strolled about the room, lighting the candle wall sconces that cast flickering golden light on the cedar walls.

The way he seemed to loom larger than life in the candlelight once again brought to mind the Beast of her youthful fairy tale. Or, Gillian considered as she glanced over at the piano, the Phantom of the Opera, perhaps.

''Something wrong with lightbulbs?''

''These are more practical.'' He blew out the long

match. "The power goes out a great deal on the island."

"You don't have a generator?"

"Of course. But there are times when I prefer candlelight."

Once again he surprised her. Gillian would not have expected a man of his obviously modern tastes and lusty male appetites to take time to consider mood lighting. Then again, perhaps there was some other reason. One they should get out into the open before things went any further.

"Or perhaps you prefer candlelight because it softens the scars on your face," she suggested. Since he'd vowed never to lie to her, she felt it important that she be equally open with him.

She saw the surprise on his face, then watched him quickly stifle it. "Some women might find my features dampen their desire."

"Some women should learn to look beyond the exterior."

"Admit it, Gillian. Aren't you secretly appalled by the changes in my physical appearance?"

"No."

"Disgusted?"

"Not at all. I'm not some fragile, overly sensitive artiste who needs to be wrapped in cotton wool, Hunter. I've played charity concerts in some of the most war-ravaged regions of the world. Physical scars don't concern me," she said quietly. "Except when they lead to emotional ones."

"But you are curious," he continued to press, as if searching out flaws.

Gillian was tempted to fudge, but honesty won out. "Of course. I'm curious about everything about you. Your work, what you've been doing since you left MIT, how you ended up here living like a very wealthy hermit—"

"How half of me got blown away."

"From what I can tell, you injured your face and lost a hand. That's not exactly half of you."

"True enough." His grin was quick, wolfish and designed to insult. "Don't worry, baby, all the parts you need to be concerned about are in full working order."

"You've no idea how pleased I am to hear that." Deciding they'd parried enough, she pulled out the piano bench. "And don't call me baby. My name's Gillian."

Damned if she didn't have spirit. Hunter knew her father well enough to know that George opted for bluster and threats when pushed into a corner. Her mother, on the other hand, would inevitably resort to the feminine seduction ploys she'd pulled out every time he'd showed up at the Cassidy home in Cambridge.

Gillian, who had both self-serving individuals' blood flowing in her veins, appeared to possess a very different nature.

Once again it occurred to him that the woman was turning out to be a lot tougher than she looked. A man who'd always enjoyed contrasts, Hunter was growing increasingly fascinated the more he studied her.

"Whatever you say. Gillian." He sprawled out on

the leather couch. "Play that song from the Irish coast," he commanded. "The seal one that starts out sounding like fairies dancing in the moonlight. The 'Song of the Selkies.' I like it best."

The song, inspired by an old Irish legend about creatures who were half women, half seal, and telling how they suffered when their husbands hid their skins, effectively holding them hostage and preventing them from returning to the sea, was Gillian's favorite. The fact that she and this dark, brooding man could have anything in common—other than lust—unnerved her.

"Thank you. I wrote that one."

"I know." He folded his arms behind his head.

"You do?"

"I would have figured that out even if I hadn't read the liner notes on the CD. The song's a reflection of you, Gillian. I can hear all your moods in the music," he said. "At first it's a light Derry air, then it turns sad, then stormy by degrees, making a listener feel as if he's drowning in the roiling waves of a dark sea."

She stared at him. A huge lump of emotion clogged her throat. "That's exactly what I intended," she whispered, wondering how two such seemingly dissimilar people could share such identical emotions.

"We're going to be good together, Gillian," he promised her. His words, spoken on a deep, lush voice that vibrated like a tuning fork inside her, revealed that they were on the same wavelength.

Needing escape from her tumultuous emotions, she turned toward the piano. At first her fingers were stiff. From the Maine cold, she told herself, conveniently overlooking the fact that not only was the fire going full blaze, the house also boasted central heating.

Deep down inside, Gillian knew it was nerves that had her fingers stumbling. Nerves were the reason she forgot to change keys at the first bridge, dropped the occasional sharp and neglected to lower a random flat.

But eventually the mood of the song, the emotions she'd experienced when she first wrote it, overcame her unease and the music started pouring from her fingertips.

In her mind, she heard the water—crystal streams tumbling over moss-covered rocks, the hushed sound of rain falling through the leaves of ancient oak trees, the whisper of an ebbing tide taking wet, glistening shells back to the sea, the crash of waves battering against limestone cliffs while the wind raged around her.

Gillian was a visual composer. She always started with a mental picture—some real, some from her dreams, some from fantasies. Wherever the images sprung from, she'd discovered at a young age that when she put them to music, it was as if she'd suddenly sprouted wings and was able to fly away to some magical, distant place, crossing the human earthly boundaries of time and space to the gilded realm of imagination.

Rhythms collided and melded into one another, tides of chords and arpeggios ebbing and flowing in rich, emotional soundscapes. Watching her, Hunter found her even more stunning in person than she'd been on that video. Her unwavering concentration— the sight of her bottom lip caught between her teeth—

made him ache with hunger. It was obvious that she was no longer in the room. Or his house. Or even on Castle Mountain. She'd stolen away to some rich place in her mind that he was anticipating visiting more with each passing moment.

Her percussive attack softened yet again to a more flowing rhythm, like the silent calm after a storm, before taking off again into a soaring legato run that told him the selkie had managed to find her way home, and that even as the seal-woman dove deeper and deeper beneath the Irish sea, her heart was soaring to the heavens.

Drawn to Gillian, like an ancient mariner drawn by a mythical selkie into the drowning depths of the sea, Hunter pushed himself off the couch and crossed the room to stand behind her.

She missed a note when he caressed her shoulder with his palm, but quickly recovered. Then glanced up at him over her shoulder.

"Don't stop," he murmured, as he slipped his fingers into the neckline of her scarlet sweater. "Not yet."

The cashmere was soft. Her flesh, warmed by the fire and desire, was softer. She closed her eyes, whether to shut him out or concentrate on his touch, Hunter didn't know. All he knew was that she was the most desirable woman he'd ever met and she fascinated him in ways too complex to attempt to decipher. His body felt like a rocket about to explode on the launchpad.

He tugged the sweater free of the waistband of her skirt and felt her sharp intake of breath. "Keep playing.'' He touched his mouth to the fragrant place behind her ear, the soft touch meant to both arouse and reassure.

"I don't know if I can.'' She trembled as his right hand caressed her, his fingers tracing a line of slow fire across her rib cage, up her side, the hollow beneath her arm. "Oh!'' She breathed a soft sound—part sigh, part moan—as he cupped her breast.

"You can.'' When he kissed his way down her neck, she tilted her head back, offering him access to her throat, where her pulse pounded like percussive bass chords. "You will.''

When she felt the hook snare the button at the waist of her skirt, Gillian's fingers faltered and her mind went as clear as glass.

"I can't remember what comes next.'' Heaven help her, she'd be hard-pressed to recall her own name right now.

"Don't worry about it. Just play anything that comes to mind.'' He was lowering the skirt's zipper, tooth by treacherous tooth. "While we explore what kind of music we make together.''

9

IT SEEMED SHE WAS UNABLE to deny this man anything. She wanted to please him, in part, Gillian thought, to yet again prove to him that she'd deserved a second look thirteen years ago. The problem was, of course, that in order to please Hunter, she'd have to surrender the autonomy she'd always prided herself on, choosing instead obedience. But, she reminded herself, it was, after all, her choice. And such surrender would only be temporary.

Gillian began moving her fingers over the keys again, aimlessly, the music coming solely from her heart. Notes tumbled over one another; long treble runs tangling with thrumming bass chords that reverberated in that hot, damp place between her legs.

As if in response to her silent plea, his right hand eased into the open placket of her skirt, stroking over the bone of her hip, moving lower still.

"Spread your legs a bit for me, Gillian." When she did as instructed, his fingers played their own symphony in the silken curls at the juncture of her thighs. "Now close your eyes. And try not to move."

She drew in a sharp breath as his fingers slipped into her with a silky wet ease. First one. Then another. A feverish tide rose in her, causing her to inadvertently move her hips toward that wicked, clever hand, seeking more.

"Hunter—" her fingers trembled, discordant notes slurred "—please…"

Unable to think about music while her body felt as taut as a piano wire, she gave up any attempt at playing and grabbed his hand, pressing it tighter against her in a mute attempt to satisfy this ruthless, pounding need.

She was flowing over his hand, like sun-warmed honey. Her ragged plea caused Hunter's own needs to flare higher even as a dark masculine power surged through him. He knew he could take her further, deeper, showing her the exhilaration found in the experience of pure sexual sensation.

"You're all I've been thinking about." His words, rough and ragged, scorched his throat. A ruthless stroke of his thumb against the hooded tangle of nerves hidden in the slick wet lips made her cry out. Her eyes, darkened with a blend of surprise and pleasure, those same expressive eyes that had fueled so many lustful dreams, flew open.

"I've thought about you like this." Without giving her time to recover, he pulled her from the wooden bench, held her against him and stripped the sweater over her head as he had that first night, flinging it away.

"Hot." His tongue created a trail of fire around the dusky areola. "Hungry." His teeth caught her taut nipple and tugged, drawing a ragged moan. Hunter could tell that her mind was shutting down, letting her body—and him—take over. "Mine."

He shoved her skirt down, his touch not nearly as steady as he would have liked, lifted her from the crimson puddle, laid her on top of the piano, then unzipped the gray suede boots, which left her only in a pair of opaque gray stockings that ended high on each thigh in a way that framed her fiery red curls.

Taking his time to enjoy the sight and taste of her, he rolled the stockings with aching slowness down her legs, following the sensual path with his mouth. And then, finally, she was gloriously naked, her flesh gleaming in the glow of the candlelight like pearls.

Desperate to take her hard and fast, he continued to ruthlessly rein in his lust long enough to drink in the sight of her. She looked soft and boneless, as if she'd drunk too much wine, but since she'd only had that single glass, Hunter experienced a sense of satisfaction knowing that he was responsible for that dazed look in her eyes.

"You really are lovely."

He shook his head in mute amazement that such a warm, sensual woman could have sprung from George Cassidy's icy loins. He ran the back of his good hand down her face in a slow sweep and felt her tremble. In fear? he wondered. Or anticipation? "You don't have to be afraid of me, Gillian."

Her eyelids had fluttered closed at his touch. Now they slowly lifted, allowing him to see miniature twins of himself in her widened pupils, the flames behind him making him appear to be some creature risen from hell.

Hunter wondered if that was how she saw him. And wondered even more why he should care.

"I'm not." Her smile was faint, a bit wary still, but it touched her eyes in a way that caused a distant stir of feeling he couldn't identify. "I trust you completely, Hunter. I'm more afraid of myself." A lovely flush of color flowed from her cheeks to her breasts at this admission. "Of how I feel when you look at me the way you're looking at me now."

Hunter was wondering if she knew the power of the gift she'd just given him, when she took hold of his hand and pressed it against her rosy breast. Beneath his palm, her heart fluttered like a wild bird. "Of how I feel when you touch me."

She shivered when his thumb brushed against her nipple. Sighed when he replaced his hand with his mouth.

"I like looking at you." He lifted his head and drank in the sight of her again, looking flushed and wanton atop the piano, her damp flesh glistening in the firelight, her feet unable to reach the floor, her legs open, moisture glistening like early morning dew on her silken curls.

"I like touching you." He skimmed a fingertip down a milky thigh. "And I especially like tasting you."

He touched his tongue to a pale blue vein revealed by her milky, Irish-pale skin and was vaguely surprised when there was no hiss of steam. When his teeth nipped at that fragrant flesh, she cried out, a sharp sound of pleasure mixed with pain.

"Please, Hunter."

Gillian had never begged for any man in her life. But as need coiled tightly inside her, she realized that was because she'd never met a man she wanted in the way she wanted Hunter St. John. Never met a man who could make her willing to toss away a lifetime of sexual restraint in order to learn the secrets her body had been hungering for since her first night on Castle Mountain.

Hunter knew those secrets. She'd witnessed it in his hot, hungry eyes as they'd looked at her, seeing beyond her clothing, even, she'd thought, past her tingling skin, to some hidden feminine place deep inside her.

She'd felt it in his hand, which revealed a familiarity with the female body that caused needs to well up inside her at the same time she hated all the other women he'd touched in such an intimate fashion.

The hook that had replaced his left hand glinted dangerously in the firelight as he captured an erect nipple between the prongs, delicately, but in a way that would have prevented her from moving, if she'd wanted to. Which, heaven help her, she didn't.

As he watched her in the steady, unblinking way a diving falcon might watch a small gray mouse, Gillian understood that this was a test, that he was searching out disgust on her face. He wouldn't find it.

"Please," she repeated on a soft, thready tone. "I want you, Hunter."

I need you. The words went unspoken, but there was no need to articulate them.

The prongs opened. Closed. "Soon." Opened again. "You're a woman of virtues, Gillian. Surely you've acquired the virtue of patience."

Only this morning Gillian could have assured him that patience had always been one of her strongest traits. Now it seemed to have scattered like dry leaves attacked by hurricane-force winds.

The touch of that cold point of steel against her burning flesh proved unbelievingly erotic, and although she'd always considered herself a self-controlled woman, Gillian discovered what she suspected only a few women could ever know, that sexual surrender to the right man—a man you could trust absolutely—could be glorious.

The fact that Hunter was still fully dressed while she was naked was strangely, undeniably exciting. When he spread her legs wider, so far apart she felt a faintly painful tug in her hip joints, she felt no embarrassment. No shame. Only pride and an age-old feminine power that she could be the cause of the hunger that was written in bold script across his normally inscrutable face.

"Lovely," he murmured again. The tip of the hook tugged on the blazing nest of hair. Gillian didn't flinch. But she did moan as he knelt down between her legs and with deft fingers parted the deep rose flesh of her outer lips, revealing the paler petal-pink opening.

When his tongue flicked over those tingling lips, it caused such a spark of exquisite pain that Gillian gasped and began to tremble like a woman in the grips of a fever.

"Stay still," he ordered huskily, as if she could control the demands of her mutinous body.

His touch was ecstasy. Agony. Alternating strict

commands with lush compliments and warm endearments, he seemed ruthless in his need to pleasure her—fondling, licking, sucking, biting, ravishing her with mouth and hand, bring her to a seemingly never-ending series of orgasms that racked her body.

The more Gillian gave into Hunter, the more control she surrendered, the more she came. Over and over. Until she was slick and wet from her own juices and aroused anew by the musky scent of sex rising from between her splayed legs.

She couldn't possibly take any more, she thought as he lifted her hips off the piano and pressed her mound against his mouth. When his tongue thrust deeply into the moist cleft, Gillian gasped for breath and felt her blood pounding in her heart, her ears, that burning place between her thighs.

It was too much.

At the same time, it was not enough. Because even as yet another series of convulsions shuddered through her, Gillian still wanted Hunter. All of him.

Across the room a log shifted, but with her mind clouded by smoke and haze and her body battered by an increasing crescendo of sexual sensations she could feel all the way to the marrow of her bones, Gillian was only distantly aware of the resultant flare of sparks.

Fond schoolgirl memories of that ancient crush she'd had on an older man spun away, while her future seemed aeons in the distance. There was only now. Only this glorious, shimmering presence with Hunter.

At this suspended moment in time, there was nothing he could have asked for that she would not have willingly given. The idea that she, a woman who'd always insisted on absolute control in all parts of her life, should feel this way both intrigued and excited Gillian. She knew she'd have to give the mystery more serious thought. Later, when she could think again.

Hunter realized that he'd won the victory he'd been seeking. Gillian's mind, her heart, her lush, fragrant body, all were his for the taking. Even as he was pleased by her open-hearted gift of absolute submission—it had, after all, been his intention to tame her, to break down all her barriers of independence until she was unconditionally his—he was discovering he'd not remained unaffected by her uncensored response.

As his body had hardened, his own heart had strangely softened. She'd touched him. In a way that could prove a threat, a way he'd have to examine. When he could think again.

But for now, driven by sexual needs stronger than the forces of nature that had formed the towering cliffs on which his house was perched, he released her just long enough to strip off his clothes and sheathe himself.

Then, with a single hard thrust he surged into her, deep and hard, driven by her breathless cries, the feel of her inner muscles, contracting, drawing him in.

"Put your legs around me, Gillian."

His voice, rough and guttural and nearly incoherent, was unfamiliar to his own ears. But somehow Gillian managed to understand him and she did as instructed, her hands fretting up and down his back, her unlacquered nails digging into his flesh in a way that fed his lust even further.

He hammered into her, again and again, hot flesh slapping against hot flesh, her soft cries muffled by his ravenous mouth as it ate into hers, his tongue thrusting between her parted lips in rhythm with his bucking hips.

A red haze shimmered in front of Hunter's eyes. His movements quickened. Deepened. And then he was coming, in a hot, torrential release that had him shouting out. The single word that was wrenched out of his chest to reverberate around the red cedar walls of the room was her name: Gillian.

An instant later, she followed him over the edge.

Hunter had no idea how long they lay there, her half on, half off the piano, him collapsed on top of her, his heart pounding, his body too drained to move. It could have been minutes. Hours. It felt like an eternity.

The ravenous hunger that had escalated with each passing day had finally, at least for now, been temporarily sated. He could stay like this forever. Buried inside her, feeling her soft feminine curves yielding to his harsher angles, her pearly skin, which had been fever-hot, now cooling, like a moist summer mist against his. He nuzzled at her neck and breathed in a flowery fragrance that mingled with the redolent, evocative musk of sex.

Hunter couldn't recall a time when he'd felt more satisfied. More fulfilled. Which was exactly why he had to move away.

She murmured a faint complaint as he eased out of

her. Her legs hung limply over the edge of the Steinway, her arms at her sides, her eyes closed, dark-
looking like strands of gold and copper silk against
her still flushed cheeks.

There were marks on her pale flesh, faint purple
bruises that were mute evidence of the passion they'd
shared. Hunter knew that he should feel guilty for
having put them there, but couldn't, since they were,
in their own way, like a brand. As if he'd burned his
name into her silken flesh.

His satisfaction at that idea was quickly dampened
when he viewed the dark smears marring the smooth
white flesh of her inner thighs.

"Gillian." He touched a still glistening smear with
a fingertip.

Her only response was a sleepy murmur that was
more purr than proper answer.

"Gillian," he repeated, cupping her cheek in his
palm. "Open your eyes."

Another faint protest. But she did as instructed.

"You were a virgin."

It was not a question, but Gillian answered it, anyway. "Yes."

"Why the hell didn't you tell me?"

She sighed. "Would it have made a difference?"
she asked as she propped herself up on her elbows.
"Would you have changed your mind about bringing
me here?"

"No." He'd promised he wouldn't lie to her, and
whatever else might be said about him, Hunter had
always prided himself on being a man of his word.
"But I would have done things differently."

"Oh? How?"

Having never been one to indulge in long, heartfelt conversation after sex, Hunter was finding this topic more unpalatable than most.

"I would have been more careful with you. Taken you with more finesse."

She stretched, in an unconsciously seductive way that reminded him of a sleek, satisfied cat. "I thought you showed amazing finesse."

"I managed some restraint in the beginning," he allowed. "But I ended up taking you like some kind of animal."

"Oh, that."

Her smile was slow and decidedly sensual, giving Hunter a very good idea of what Eve must have looked like after she and Adam had shared bites of that serpent's shiny red forbidden apple.

"Actually, Hunter, I thought that was wonderful." The siren's smile darkened her eyes, turning them from Irish moss to emeralds. "Thrilling, actually."

He was going to have to send her away, Hunter decided yet again. She was too enticing. Too appealing. Too damn dangerous. But first...

He scooped her up from the piano, threw her over his shoulder and walked out of the room.

"What about our clothes?" she asked, seeming as unfazed by her upside-down position as she'd been about everything else he'd thrown at her these past days. "We can't just leave them here. Mrs. Adams—"

"Is well paid not to notice," he said as he strode down the hall to the master bedroom suite, where he plunked her unceremoniously on the closed lid of the commode while he ran the water in the oversize tub.

The water streaming from the wide swan's-neck tap was hot; he tossed in a handful of herbal bath salts he'd bought specifically with her in mind and soon they were surrounded by fragrant steam.

"Hunter?" she asked as he moved the soft-as-silk Egyptian cotton washcloth over her bloodied thighs.

"What?" Self-recrimination made his tone sharper than he'd intended.

"I know you don't care about image. Or your reputation." She bit her bottom lip as she looked up at him through a thick fringe of lashes. "But I do. And I don't think I'll be able to face Mrs. Adams tomorrow morning knowing that she knows we were having an orgy in your library."

Hunter wondered how it was that even after what they'd just shared, she could remain such an innocent. "It wasn't exactly an orgy, Gillian. Besides, Mrs. Adams is an employee. It's none of her business what we do. Or where."

She didn't exactly seem won over by his argument. "Please?" When the touch of her hand on his arm brought back the memory of those slender fingers against his burning flesh, Hunter felt himself giving in.

"All right. If it'll make you feel better, I'll go get them."

"Thank you, Hunter." Her smile could have lit up the entire island for the entire winter. "That's very nice of you."

Both touched and irritated by the wave of emotion

sparked by that dazzling smile, Hunter cupped her chin and gave her a hard, tooth-grinding, punishing kiss.

"I told you, baby," he reminded her on a growl, when they finally came up for air. "I'm never nice."

That stated, he stood up and strode from the bathroom.

"Hunter?" She called out to him as he reached the doorway.

He shot her a frustrated glance over his shoulder. "What now?"

"My name isn't baby."

Because he wanted to laugh, he merely shrugged his shoulders and left the room. But even as he reminded himself that Gillian Cassidy was turning out to be trouble with a capital *T,* he found her impossible to resist.

Although he suspected very little got past the eagle-eyed Mrs. Adams, he retrieved their clothes from the library. Then, as he succumbed to temptation and joined Gillian in the tub, Hunter tried to ignore the uneasy feeling that he wasn't really sinking into the fragrant hot water, but into quicksand.

GILLIAN FOUGHT THROUGH the fog of sleep filled with erotic memories, some real, others born in dreams so vivid she wondered if some of them could have actually occurred. As her mind gradually cleared, she wasn't all that surprised when she woke up and found that Hunter had gone. Disappointed but not surprised.

"After all, he does have work to do," she murmured, reluctantly leaving the tangled sheets that still carried Hunter's scent.

The fire had died sometime during the night; the former blaze had burned down to embers as cold as the lonely bed. "He can't stay in bed all day just because you've discovered that making love just might be your favorite thing to do."

No. Not making love, Gillian reminded herself. "It was only sex." She stretched from side to side, trying to work out the unfamiliar kinks. "Great sex. But that's all it was. Love had nothing at all to do with it."

At least on his part. But she feared that somehow, between when she'd barged into his office and the time, just before dawn, when he'd given her a kiss so sweet and tender it had almost made her weep, she'd begun to fall in love with him.

"It's merely the situation." Continuing the little pep talk, she walked across the room and opened the draperies. "He's set up a ridiculously erotic situation. There's probably not a woman in the world who could resist falling a little under the spell."

That thought, meant to comfort, did just the opposite as Gillian wondered how many women Hunter had made love to—"had sex with," she corrected again sternly—in this room. In this bed.

If there was one thing Gillian was certain of since arriving on Castle Mountain, it was that a man with Hunter's sexual skills must be an inveterate seducer of women.

"Well, at least the piano may have been a first." Gillian sighed at the realization that a few days under the same roof with Hunter would have her foolishly grasping at such weak straws.

Along with the storm that Gillian and Hunter had created last night, a blizzard had blown in from the mainland. The entire world was engulfed in a white blanket; more snow was battering against the glass wall. It was definitely a day to stay indoors.

A day to stay in bed, she thought, feeling her hormones spike dangerously as remembered sensual images caused a slow burn deep inside her. As she went into the bathroom, which had its share of erotic memories, Gillian wondered, yet again, what on earth she'd gotten herself into.

After showering, she returned to the bedroom, opened the top bureau drawer to retrieve a sweater and found it filled with the lingerie Hunter had taken away that first night. Even as she understood that this was his way of maintaining control by rewarding her for last night's submission, she was inexorably drawn to the scanty bits of lace so different from anything she'd ever owned. She ran her fingers through them, enjoying the feel of silk against her fingertips, the slick of cool satin. Then she smiled.

Like everything else about Hunter's home, the lingerie almost seemed to be imbued with magic. She'd no sooner put it on than Gillian felt her spirits lift. She was humming as she entered the kitchen.

"Good morning," she greeted Mrs. Adams, receiving a grunt in return. Refusing to allow the taciturn woman to spoil this special day, she smiled and said, "I'm surprised to see you here today."

"Don't know why you should be." The housekeeper cracked an egg on the side of a blue ceramic bowl. "It's my job, after all."

"But the storm's so bad."

"Ben's truck has four-wheel drive. It'll go near anywhere."

Gillian walked over to the kitchen window, looking out at the drifts that were beginning to pile up against the glass. She wondered if her cat was out there, wet and cold and hungry. That thought caused a little pall to drift over her good mood.

"Well, I'm sure Dr. St. John appreciates your devotion to duty, but I can't believe he'd expect you to come out in a blizzard."

"T'weren't a blizzard when we left our place. Though the snow was sure enough starting to pile up when Dr. St. John left."

"Left?" Gillian turned back toward the housekeeper. "Dr. St. John went out?"

"Ayuh."

That came as a surprise, given his seemingly reclusive lifestyle. "Did he tell you where he went?"

"Can't say as he did." Butter sizzled hotly in a cast-iron skillet. Normally the fragrance would have stimulated Gillian's appetite. But not now. "Though it'd be my guess he went over to the brain factory."

"Brain factory?"

"His laboratory."

"Oh." Gillian cradled the mug in her hands and took another sip of coffee. "I thought his lab was here in the house."

"That's where he works most times," Mrs. Adams allowed. "But he's on staff at the brain factory."

"Is it far away?"

Mrs. Adams's bony shoulders lifted in a shrug. "Not much that's far away around these parts. It's a small island. The brain factory's on the other side. The town's sort of in the middle." She poured the eggs into the pan and began energetically stirring them around with a fork.

"Still, that's quite a trip in a storm like this." Gillian went from feeling abandoned to fearing for Hunter's safety.

"Weather Service says it'll be a short, quick blow. 'Course, forecasts are wrong as often as right this time of year. But you needn't worry about Dr. St. John, since he won't be driving back today."

"He won't?" Her heart sank.

"Told me I wasn't to worry about making him supper tonight or tomorrow. Said he'd call after that and let me know his plans."

"I see." All too well. Hunter couldn't have made his point more clear if he'd written it across the bathroom mirror in bold black paint.

Mrs. Adams flipped the scrambled eggs onto a plate and put the plate down on the table. "I suppose you'll be wanting some extra bacon. For that fool wild cat."

"I'd appreciate that, Mrs. Adams."

The woman's huff told Gillian she'd suspected nothing less. It also suggested that she thought Dr. St. John's houseguest was crazy.

Gillian couldn't blame her. She was, after all, rapidly coming to the same conclusion herself.

10

IT WASN'T WORKING. The plan, which had seemed logical enough when Hunter had finally abandoned the warm comfort of the bed he'd shared with Gillian two days ago was turning out to be a bust.

He'd never thought of himself as a particularly greedy man. Granted, the wealth that came from his work was a nice perk, and if the government wanted to write him an obscenely large check to stake a claim to his research, he certainly wasn't about to turn it down. But everything else—including the house he'd designed down to the last nail—was just gravy.

So long as he had enough funds to keep his work going, he wouldn't care if he woke up tomorrow to find it all gone.

As for relationships with the opposite sex, even prior to the bombing, he'd preferred brief, uncomplicated affairs with women who were no more interested than he was in any kind of permanent relationship. These past years on the island with Toni had been more convenience than emotion, friendly lust that scratched an itch for them both.

He liked Toni. A lot. He liked her mind, her body, her penchant for sexual adventure. He also liked the fact that he could get caught up in his work for days or weeks at a time and she wouldn't get her feelings hurt or feel abandoned. After all, she felt the same way. They were comfortably compatible, neither believing in, nor wanting, any happily-ever-after type of commitment.

Still, he couldn't help being relieved that she'd left the island for a research trip to the National Institutes of Health in Atlanta. He knew she'd understand why it would be awkward to sleep with her while he had another woman living in his house. But Toni was a highly intuitive woman and he didn't want anyone realizing that his feelings for Gillian had unexpectedly become more complex than merely sexual.

Hell. Only two weeks ago things had been going along well. Better than well. After years of compiling data, he'd been crunching the numbers and had felt as if he'd been close to a breakthrough when Toni had shown up at his house with that damn tape.

Ever since that evening, his mind had been dominated by thoughts about Gillian Cassidy.

He'd hoped that if he got away from the house—from her—he'd be able to concentrate and focus on his work. But as the computer hummed away, Hunter stood by the window of his laboratory, staring out at the swirling snow and thinking of Gillian on the other side of the woods.

He wondered if she was still lying in bed, still tangled in the sheets that had finally begun to cool when he'd left before dawn that morning. Wondered if she was taking a bath in the Jacuzzi tub. Wondered if she was thinking of him.

Was she regretting giving up her virginity to a man

who hadn't particularly welcomed it and had treated her with less tenderness than the situation had called for? But how the hell had he been supposed to know the woman was far more innocent than her sensual music had led him to believe?

He jammed his hands into the pockets of his jeans and reminded himself that Gillian was a grown woman. She'd known before coming to the island what would be expected of her, and even if she hadn't totally believed he was serious, he'd certainly made himself perfectly clear since her arrival.

So why the hell was he experiencing this unexpected guilt? And another, even more unsettling feeling he couldn't quite put a name to?

"Damn," he muttered as he glared out at the swirling white snow.

"Numbers not crunching well?" a masculine voice behind him asked as Dylan strolled into the office.

"The work's going well enough." He shrugged with more casualness than he felt. "Actually, it's turning out better than expected."

"Then it must be a woman who's got you looking like a ticked-off lion with a thorn in your paw."

"You couldn't begin to imagine," Hunter said dryly.

Dylan laughed with obvious delight. "If I didn't know that you weren't a man given to entanglements, I'd suspect that the tables had been turned and the lovely red-haired songstress has snared the hunter."

At first Hunter was a bit surprised that Dylan knew it was Gillian that Ben had brought to his house. Then realized he should have expected it. Any visitor to

Castle Mountain was bound to be noticed right away, especially once tourist season had passed. Especially a high-profile visitor like Gillian Cassidy.

"It's complicated," he muttered, jamming his hands deeper into his pockets as he glared back out the window.

"It usually is, when a female's concerned," Dylan said with the blithe attitude of a happily married man. "I take it your visitor has you dancing to her tune?"

Hunter frowned. He wasn't prepared to talk about Gillian. Not even with Dylan. Not when he hadn't yet figured out what he was feeling.

"Did you drop by to play Dear Abby?"

"No." The smile faded from Dylan's eyes. "You have a visitor."

"Oh?" He wondered if Gillian had actually managed to talk Ben into driving her here and wondered, if she had, why he didn't feel any irritation at her invading his sanctuary.

"It's the general," Dylan said. "He's currently cooling his heels in the reception area."

Hunter shook his head. Just what he needed to top off a less-than-perfect day. He wondered how the man had made his way here from the mainland in such lousy weather, then, remembering the many tales he'd heard over the years about his covert activities going all the way back to the final days of Vietnam, he realized that General Alexander Stonewall Lee wasn't going to allow snow—even a near blizzard—to interfere with a mission.

He cursed, then sighed with resignation. Lee was, after all, the man who signed his checks.

"Send him in."

The general possessed the bearing of a man for whom military service was a birthright. As he entered the office on a strong, confident stride that brought to mind a conquering army, Hunter could almost imagine him standing at full parade attention in his mother's womb.

"I wasn't expecting you." Hunter opened a maple cabinet and took out the bottle of Wild Turkey he kept on hand for the general's visits.

"I wasn't expecting to be here." Snow glistened in his silver hair as General Lee took off his overcoat, boasting four gold stars on the shoulder epaulets, and hung it on the brass rack. "I try to make it a policy not to travel north of the Mason-Dixon line after Thanksgiving."

"That must make it difficult to wage war in the northern regions," Hunter suggested dryly.

"Which is why I got myself a transfer to the Pentagon," the general said as he took the crystal glass Hunter held out to him. "Granted, one would never move to D.C. for the weather, but at least it's not as inhospitable as this place."

He glared out at the sleet hammering against the window. "If you have to live on a damn island, why couldn't you have chosen one in the Caribbean?"

Since the debacle with George Cassidy, Hunter always thoroughly investigated everyone with whom he worked. His research on the general had revealed the man was a miserable sailor. Which made it all the more surprising that he'd risk coming out here on Ben

Adams's mail packet on a day that the sea was rough enough to make even the most hardy seasick.

"The island suits me." Hunter sat down in one of the black swivel chairs. "You didn't come all this way to give me a weather report. What's so important to have you braving a stormy Atlantic to come to our little back of beyond?"

"The Pentagon has received intelligence regarding recent rumors of outside interests in your project from various terrorist groups."

"Isn't military intelligence an oxymoron?" When the general's granite face didn't so much as crack a faint smile, Hunter shrugged and glanced down at the hook that had taken the place of his left hand. "So why don't you tell me something I don't know? Besides, you're running a little behind. Van Horn's already passed on the news that I've made the latest hit list."

The general scowled at the mention of the State Department bureaucrat. "Those guys at State wouldn't know a terrorist if he showed up at their offices and bit them on their collective asses...."

"There are also rumors that you're close to completion."

He might not have any use for Van Horn, but the two men shared the same motivation in making the trip from the mainland out to the middle of nowhere.

"Closer than I was last year," Hunter agreed, not eager to volunteer information even to this man, who possessed the highest level of military clearance. "But I still have some work to do," he said, giving the general the same line he'd told the emissary from State.

"Needless to say, we're concerned about security."

"Short of moving this lab to some other galaxy, I doubt if I could find a more remote research location," Hunter pointed out.

"I won't argue with that. But the Joint Chiefs decided that we should take another check of your security measures."

"Never hurts to check," Hunter said agreeably even as he ground his teeth. So much for getting any work done, he considered, conveniently overlooking the fact that he'd already blown most of the day with thoughts of Gillian.

Five long hours later, the general announced himself satisfied with the security measures at the brain factory. He was, however, less than pleased when Hunter, pointing out that he'd been keeping the committee informed with quarterly reports, refused to give him a hands-on demonstration of the secret project. With a last warning for Hunter to watch his back, he left.

"Surely he's not actually going to try to get back to the mainland tonight?" Dylan asked as the two men watched the SUV the general had somehow managed to round up drive away.

"He's spending the night at the Gray Gull in town," Hunter said. "Then, if the weather lets up, I suppose he'll take Ben Adams's mail boat back to the mainland tomorrow."

Hunter knew that the polite thing to do would have

been to invite the man to stay at the house and save him the trip into town. He didn't for two reasons, the first being that Gillian's presence at the house might raise questions he had no intention of answering. The second reason was that he didn't like the general any more than he liked Van Horn. Having never been known for his manners, he put the general out of his mind.

Night came early to this part of the country in winter, and as the gray sky darkened, Hunter considered spending another night right here on the leather office sofa. It crossed his mind that he'd rather face an entire band of terrorists armed with hand grenades and automatic weapons than try to make casual conversation with Gillian.

After obsessing over it a helluva lot more than he liked, Hunter realized he couldn't hide from her forever. Besides, if past behavior was any example, she might actually try to track him down here. Not wanting to take the chance on her risking her life just because he'd turned into a coward overnight, he came to the reluctant conclusion that he might as well go home.

Two days after her glorious night with Hunter, Gillian was in the library, trying to keep her mind on composing the piece that had been humming through her head since she'd woken up to find him gone and the world draped in white.

Proving that the Weather Service could, indeed, be wrong, the storm had not blown over. Indeed, the snow had continued to fall from the slate sky. At times the sleet driven against the wall of windows sounded as though the house were being pelted with stones. Other times, the wind would die down and flakes would float from the slate-gray sky like fluffy goose down, almost as if the gods were engaged in a pillow fight over the world.

The weather had finally turned fierce enough to keep Mrs. Adams away. Just before the phones had gone out, the housekeeper had called to inform Gillian that she'd slipped on her icy front steps. Overriding Gillian's concern, she'd briskly informed her that the doctor said her ankle wasn't broken but badly sprained, and he had instructed her to stay off it for several days. Since the freezer was stocked with food, neither she nor Dr. St. John need worry about going hungry.

"If Dr. St. John decides to return anytime soon from the brain factory," she'd tacked on, making it sound as if Gillian shouldn't hold her breath.

And she wasn't, dammit, Gillian told herself now. Her fingers played over the keys as images of falling snow over frozen rivers and storm-tossed seas swirled in her mind.

At least the winter wonderland she could view from every room in the house was providing inspiration. The only problem was, whenever the music began to flow, her emotions would go spinning straight to the man responsible for her being here on this remote island in the first place.

"It's not enough that he's taken over my dreams," she muttered as she banged out a series of frustrated, crashing chords. "Now he's messing up my work."

She sighed, gave up for now and went over to stand by the glass wall. The feathery snow had turned back into stone pellets, and the wind wailing like a lost ghost down the chimney had the effect on her tangled nerves of fingernails scraping down a chalkboard. She was about to turn on the CD player to try to drown it out when another sound caught her attention. A wail that sounded more like a human than any unearthly spirit.

"No, not a person," she corrected herself, straining to listen closer. The faint wail was ragged and plaintive. Like a cat. Her cat.

Her heartbeat picked up. She leaned forward, her nose literally pressed against the window as she peered out into the driving snow. There it went again! Though she couldn't see him, Gillian knew that it had to be the cat both Hunter and Mrs. Adams had assured her was feral.

"Wild or not, he's in trouble."

Unable to resist the wretched cries of despair, she ran to the kitchen, pulled on the outerwear Hunter had bought for her and, heedless of her own safety, went rushing out into the storm.

HUNTER HAD DRIVEN about a mile through the white swirls when he came across a fallen tree limb across the road. It wasn't that big, and normally he would have merely driven around it, but the blinding snow obscured the edge of the cliff. Cursing, he abandoned the warm interior of the Suburban, swearing again when the cold wind slapped his face.

He'd nearly managed to drag the tree out of the

way when he was aware of something—or someone—behind him. He turned, and before he could straighten, he saw something metal. His parka ripped. There was a burning sensation in his upper arm.

Since high school Hunter had studied aikido, a form of martial arts that taught defense without weapons. He enjoyed honing the discipline of mind and body. Banking his self-disgust at having fallen for such an obvious trap, he turned his attention to staying alive.

He and his black-ski-masked opponent were fairly evenly matched. On some distant level, Hunter almost admired the man's strength and his moves, which were, he admitted, a stage above his own, but his own rigid emotional discipline seemed marginally superior.

They battled in eerie silence in the swirling white world, their movements rhythmic, almost balletic. Years of self-discipline kept Hunter's mind cool and focused. Unlike the letter bomb, which he'd always thought a cowardly way to try to kill someone, this attempt on his life seemed, in some abstract way, little more than a training session.

Then, as he dodged another lunge, the tautly held reins of mental control slipped. Just a little, but enough to allow his thoughts to go to Gillian. Obviously, if this man had known Hunter was at the brain factory, he'd also have known that she was alone in the house. Alone and, despite all his security measures, ultimately defenseless.

Hunter had no doubt that he could handle his attacker. But what if there were more? What if there were others, even now, at his house terrifying her? Harming her?

An ugly blend of terror and fury twisted in his gut and ripped at his scattering control. Hunter abandoned finesse. With a roar that echoed through the Maine woods, he hurled his body at his attacker.

HAVING FOLLOWED THE CAT'S cries to the clam flats below the cliff, Gillian was seriously rethinking her decision when she spotted it, just a few feet away. The tide was coming in, the whitecaps riding atop the roiling waves looking like ice floes. The thunder of the incoming sea provided a deep bass accompaniment to the shriek of the wind and the yowls of the cat she'd now come to think of as hers. Sleet stung her face like needles.

Lowering her head, Gillian doggedly made her way over the kelp, struggling over driftwood and flotsam that had been washed ashore, slipping on rocks, once losing her balance and falling to her knees.

It was while she was kneeling on the wet gray sand that she watched the cat disappear into a narrow cave, more fissure than cavern, carved into the side of the cliff by eons of wind and water.

Muttering a curse, she pushed herself back to her feet and stumbled over to the cave, where inside, lying on a bed of seaweed, she found three wet balls of fur.

"Kittens." Gillian shook her head and looked over at the cat who was standing over her offspring with obvious maternal pride. "So, I guess this means you're not a he after all."

The cat's response was short and sharp and suggested that they not waste time discussing the obvious. As water lapped dangerously close to the kittens, Gillian realized that time was definitely running out.

She scooped the kittens up, sticking one in her left parka pocket and two in the right, which left them a little crowded, but since she didn't have either the time or the energy to make two trips, Gillian decided that after months jostling around together in the cat's womb, they should be accustomed to close quarters.

Another wave washed over her boots. "Dammit, you're going to owe me," she warned the cat, who'd already turned and was headed out of the cave, tail raised like a tricolored banner. "Big time."

AFTER HE'D SENT his attacker flying silently, fatally off the edge of the cliff, Hunter made his way home, his head filled with unpalatable images of Gillian in danger. When he ran into the house, the note he found on the kitchen table did nothing to ease his mind.

It was written in a neat, disciplined convent schoolgirl script that was so opposite to her passionate nature it almost made him smile.

Dear Hunter,
In case you return while I'm gone, I'm out with the cat. He's in trouble and I couldn't leave him to the elements.

Gillian

P.S. I hope your work at the brain factory went well.

As he skimmed the brief note, Hunter's blood turned even icier than the weather outside. Wondering which of them was crazier, he or Gillian, he waded back out into the storm.

The woman was too damn softhearted for her own good. Hunter couldn't think of a single person he knew who'd behave in such an asinine, potentially fatal manner.

He followed her footprints, which were rapidly disappearing, for what seemed an eternity. A dreadful wet, cold eternity. The snow thickened, decreasing visibility. The sea crashed onto the shore, turning the usually wide stretch of beach into a sliver of flotsam-strewn sand.

When he caught sight of the cardinal-red parka, a single vivid color in a vast gray-and-white world, he let out a breath he'd been unaware of holding. Along with a string of pungent curses.

"What the hell do you think you're doing?" He grasped her shoulders, and because he couldn't decide whether to crush her to him and never let go, or to shake some sense into her, he did neither. "Don't you realize you could be washed out to sea?"

His words were whipped away by the wind, but Gillian had no problem understanding his meaning. She could feel the hook digging into her shoulder, even through the thick parka; his breath was like puffs of white ghosts between them.

"You don't understand—" she began to explain, having to shout to be heard over the rumble of surf.

"I understand that you're a damn idiot!" Hunter realized he'd have to apologize for the harsh words.

Later. When they were safely back at the house. And after she apologized for scaring the hell out of him with her cockamamie behavior. "Now, let's get out of here before you end up getting us both killed."

Seeming to understand that he was in no mood for an argument, Gillian simply nodded, then let him half drag her back up the rocky path to the top of the cliff, then to the house.

Compared to the near-arctic temperatures outdoors, the heat of the kitchen hit Gillian like a blast furnace. Before Hunter could slam the door, the cat sprinted into the room and began doing figure eights between her legs, its yowls seeming to increase in volume.

"What, exactly, did you think you were doing?" he demanded again.

"I'm sorry I wasn't here when you got back, Hunter, but it really was an emergency."

"A cat emergency?"

Now that the adventure was behind her, the seriousness of the risk she'd taken came crashing down on Gillian. White dots resembling the falling snow began to swirl in front of her eyes. Holding on to the edge of the table for balance, she sank down onto a chair.

As her vision cleared, she looked up at Hunter, who was standing over her, his glare as hard as the granite cliffs.

But there was something else in his dark eyes. Something she'd have to think about once her blood warmed and her teeth stopped chattering.

"Kittens," she corrected him, forcing the word past frozen lips.

She retrieved them from the deep coat pockets, one at a time, placing them on the floor at her feet. Even with their eyes tightly closed, they managed to make their way on wobbly legs to their mother, who, now that the crisis was over, had gone back to ignoring Gillian.

Hunter's incredulous look went from Gillian, to the kittens, who were being tongue-bathed by their mother, then back to Gillian.

Then he did something more surprising than anything he'd done thus far. He threw back his head and roared with laughter.

Later, when she would look back on things and wonder how they'd gone so terribly wrong, Gillian would realize that this was the moment she'd truly fallen in love with Hunter St. John.

"I missed you," she murmured, pushing herself out of the chair on legs nearly as unstable as the kittens' to touch a hand to his cheek. "Terribly."

Hunter didn't respond as she'd hoped. Didn't assure her that he'd missed her, too. "You're cold," he said instead.

She couldn't help herself. She'd begun to shiver. And not from passion.

"Why don't you warm me up?"

He gave her another of those long, searching looks. Gillian could tell he was tempted. "Later," he decided. "First I'm going to run you a bath."

"That sounds wonderful."

She wasn't expecting the way he undressed her almost as if she were a child, with a heartaching tenderness, and was even more surprised when, after she'd slipped beneath the froth of bubbles, he turned to leave the bathroom.

"Aren't you joining me?"

He glanced back at her, his face granite hard, his eyes now unreadable. "I have some calls to make."

"The phones went out earlier."

"I have a shortwave radio in the lab."

"Oh." She thought about that for a moment. "It's that important?"

His jaw firmed. Despite the warmth of the water, the flash of iced fury that moved across his face chilled her blood all over again. "Yes."

With that less-than-satisfying explanation, he was gone.

11

AFTER A STEAMING HOT BATH that seemed about as close as any individual could get to heaven on earth, Gillian was back in the kitchen, wrapped in Hunter's robe and a pair of thick fuzzy socks. She'd turned down his offer of brandy, choosing cocoa instead, and was now on her second cup.

The kittens were a few feet away, in an apple box lined with thick towels.

"That was nice of you."

He skimmed an uncaring glance she didn't believe for a moment over the infant-blind kittens. "Mrs. Adams would have had my head if I let them wander all over her kitchen."

"And we both know how terrified you are of your housekeeper," Gillian said dryly.

When she'd first rescued the wet kittens, their weak, stuttering cries had tugged at her heart. Now, at the sight of them happily suckling, a maternal drive Gillian hadn't even been aware of possessing rose from somewhere deep inside her.

"You realize that you really are crazy," Hunter murmured with a slow shake of his head. The unmistakable affection in his voice kept Gillian from taking offense.

Crazy about you, she thought.

"Obviously, you've spent so many years in la-la land, you've forgotten the risks of going out in a New England blizzard," he continued sarcastically.

"I live in Monterey," she said mildly, refusing to rise to his anti-California bait. "As for going outside, I didn't have any choice."

He gave her a long, hard look. Then sighed heavily. "No, I suppose you didn't."

He reached across the table with his good hand and flicked a bit of whipped cream from her upper lip. When he licked the fluffy white cream from his fingertip, another, more immediate elemental need steamrolled over the errant maternal instincts the sight of cat and kittens had stimulated.

"I really did miss you." Gillian lifted her gaze from those enticing fingers that had played such havoc to her senses to his face. "I tried to work...I had all these wonderful melodies singing about in my mind, but you kept getting in the way."

"Am I supposed to say I'm sorry?"

"Oh, it wasn't a complaint. Just the truth." She sighed. "Sticking to the truth when a lie would be easier is one of my social flaws."

He arched a brow, inviting elaboration.

Gillian complied with the silent request, as she had so many others. "For instance, just suppose that you'd bought a new dress—"

"If I took to wearing dresses, we'd have an entirely different problem."

She giggled a little at that, which surprised her. Her childhood had not encouraged humor, and although

Deke had always been able to make her laugh, Gillian wasn't certain she'd ever giggled before.

"Don't be so literal. You know what I mean."

"Why don't you give me an example?"

"All right." She thought a moment. "A few months ago a cellist who occasionally tours with me asked if a new skirt made her thighs look too heavy. Now, I should have just said the skirt was lovely and she looked great."

"But you didn't do that."

"No. I couldn't do that. Not in good conscience."

Once again Hunter looked for any signs that she was her parents' daughter and found none. Since lies had come to Irene and George Cassidy as easily as breathing, he could only surmise that Gillian was a changeling.

"Sometimes white lies are easier," he suggested. "For everyone concerned."

He certainly didn't intend to tell her about his encounter with the knife-wielding terrorist. Thus far, he'd only shared the news with the general and Dylan, so his best—and only friend—could take his own protective measures. Just in case.

Hunter couldn't deny that he was glad the storm had knocked out the telephone; he wasn't prepared to have the island overrun with additional military personnel. As for his attacker, he figured it could be days before his body washed up on shore. With any luck, it would be torn apart and eaten by sharks first.

"Lies get so complicated," she murmured. "First you tell one, then that leads to another, and of course you have to keep track of them all and pretty soon you're tangled up in a mess of your own making.''

"What a pretty web we weave," he murmured. "So what did you tell the cellist with the chubby thighs?"

"That I thought the color didn't flatter her skin tones and that I'd seen a stunning black silk number with crystal trim in the hotel boutique that had her name on it.''

Gillian grinned at the memory. "She looked stunning. That night an undersecretary of state asked her out to dinner after the show. They're getting married in June."

"All because of a dress?"

"Oh, no. The dress was just packaging. He fell in love with my friend.'' Humor danced in her remarkable eyes. "But the dress did help get his attention in the first place.''

"Hooked the guy so she could reel him in.''

The sparkle, like sunshine on snow, faded from her eyes. "Is that how you think about love? About being hooked and reeled in?"

"Actually, I don't think about love.''

"That's sad.''

"I suppose you do?" It was a rhetorical question. Hunter already knew the answer.

"Occasionally.'' When he lifted another brow, she laughed. "All right, the fantasy of finding and spending the rest of my life with my one true love is one of my favorite things. Right up there with Christmas, chocolate—'' she glanced fondly at the box of sleeping cats ''—fluffy kittens and writing the music for a hit play on Broadway.''

''Why Broadway? You've already played at the pyramids and Stonehenge.''

''And had a glorious time at both. Especially Stonehenge. That was the most amazingly incredible experience. I could feel the magic...''

She paused, tilted her head and studied him gravely. ''I suppose that as a scientist, you don't believe in magic, either.''

''No. I don't.''

''That's too bad.'' She drew in a breath, then let it out again, as if having come to a decision. ''We're going to have to work on that,'' she said. ''Even a mad brilliant scientist needs a little magic in his life....

''And getting back to Broadway, despite what impression you have of me, I possess a fair amount of drive and ego. I've always loved musical theater, and having my name up in bright lights on the Great White Way just seems like the pinnacle of success.''

''Well, if that's what you want, I've not a single doubt you'll make that pinnacle.'' No white lies needed there, Hunter thought.

''Thank you, Hunter.'' Her smile was quick and warm. ''That's very sweet of you to say.''

''I told you, I'm—''

''Never sweet. I know. But it's not true, so I'm going to ignore any attempts you might make to try to convince me otherwise. I can, however, understand how you might resist the idea of falling in love. It makes sense that you'd try to avoid any situation that might cause your mind to wander.''

''It's been known to drift from time to time.'' Such as when he'd thought of her while fighting off his attacker, Hunter thought but did not say.

''Not for long, I'll bet.'' She paused again and seemed to be choosing her words carefully. ''I suppose you were too wrapped up in your work these past couple days to think of me.''

He sighed inwardly as he heard the naked need. Then he swore softly. ''I missed you, too,'' he admitted. He could give her that much, at least. ''More than I should have. A helluva lot more than I wanted.''

Because he looked so honestly distressed, Gillian leaned forward and placed her palm against his cheek. A muscle jerked against her fingertips. ''I know the feeling.''

A storm of emotions more overwhelming than physical need rushed through her. Because they were too new, too raw to share with Hunter, she closed her eyes briefly to keep them to herself.

What she'd managed to convince herself over the years had been a teenage crush, had, during her time on Castle Mountain, been blossoming into something much deeper. More lasting. She loved him. Truly, madly, deeply.

She also knew that he wasn't ready for such a revelation. If she were to admit to her feelings, he'd undoubtedly close back up again and hustle her out of the house and off the island as soon as the storm cleared.

Convinced she wasn't alone in her feelings, Gillian vowed to breach the self-protective barricades he'd erected over the years and rescue him from his self-imposed emotional and physical isolation.

She opened her eyes, her slow smile brimming with feminine invitation. "Do you remember when I compared this situation to Beauty and the Beast?"

"I vaguely recall something about that."

"I had the wrong fairy tale."

"Oh?"

"I've come to the conclusion that it's more along the lines of Frankenstein."

"So you consider me a monster?"

A shadow moved across his eyes, so quickly that if she hadn't been watching him carefully, Gillian would have missed it. No wonder he'd built those walls, she thought sadly, with a little hitch in her heart. She'd already discovered that he was far more sensitive, more vulnerable, than he was willing to admit, even to himself.

"No." She shook her head. "You're the doctor. Who created the monster who went amok. Ever since you made love to me—"

"Had sex," he corrected her swiftly. Firmly.

She should have known he'd balk at the *L* word. Even as she wanted more, Gillian reminded herself that patience was reputed to be a virtue.

"Ever since we had sex," she amended, "it's been almost all I've thought about."

She skimmed her fingers down the unscarred side of his face, around his harshly carved lips. Lips she could still taste. Lips she was dying to feel all over her body again.

"You're not alone there."

Gillian decided that the growled admission was a start. "Well, then. Perhaps we should begin making up for lost time."

With a brazenness she couldn't have imagined doing only a week ago, Gillian rose to her feet, slowly untied the sash of the robe, pushed it off her shoulders and allowed it to drop to the floor.

As she stood in front of him, gloriously, achingly naked, Gillian watched the stark male hunger flame in his eyes and had never felt more like a woman. Powerful. Sexy. Seductive.

He wasn't touching her—not yet—but the heat of his gaze was enough to cause her breasts to ache.

"I imagined you touching me like this." She splayed her fingers over her breasts. Her voice, low and throaty, sounded like a stranger's. An alluring, provocative stranger who could keep the interest of a man like Hunter.

"And this." As he watched with undisguised lust, her hands roamed down her torso with an erotic slowness designed to make him ache as badly as she'd been aching since she awakened after a night of lovemaking to an empty bed.

"I dreamed of cold steel against hot flesh." Her fingernail raised a pink trail at the inside of her thigh where a pearl of moisture beaded. "And how you'd soothe the sting with your mouth."

"Gillian…" His rough, ragged complaint was half moan, half warning. Sensing the wild animal raging inside him, Gillian grew even bolder, determined to cause it to break its chains.

"Did you think about it, Hunter?" Her eyes did not leave his. "Did you dream about me?"

"Yes." His growled answer sent a thrill skimming through her.

"Hot, sexy dreams?"

"Day and night."

"I'm glad." She smiled at the idea that she'd managed to slip her way into his rigidly controlled mind.

Even as she wondered what had come over her, how she'd become so blatantly wanton, so daringly licentious, she couldn't help testing Hunter's self-control just a little bit more.

"Did you wake up hard and hot and wish you were here?"

When she cupped herself between her legs, Hunter abruptly stood up, knocking his chair over. Neither of them noticed.

"What the hell do you think?" He grasped her wrist with his good hand, yanking it away from her body to press it against his. His erection, hard and ready, jerked beneath her stroking touch.

"I think you just might be as obsessed as I am."

Hunter's response to her accusation was half laugh, half groan. "I think you just may be right."

He pulled her to him, heat to heat. His mouth captured hers in a rough, demanding kiss that answered her seductiveness with primal power and made her head swim. Gillian kissed him back, her avid mouth as hungry as his.

Somehow, they made it to the bedroom, where Gillian reveled in the carnal demands of Hunter's mouth, the roughness of his hands, the force of his powerful body as he drove her deeper and deeper into the mattress, bringing her to the very edge of release, again and again, but never letting her tumble over that final razor-sharp precipice.

"Dammit, Hunter..." No longer playing the role of submissive, Gillian raked her nails over the taut muscles of his damp back. "I can't take any more."

"You can." He was feasting on her, as a man might devour a ripe, juicy summer plum. "You will."

His mouth scorched its way up her body again. Gillian thought she heard the hiss of her skin sizzle when he dipped a kiss into her navel. He caressed her breasts to a pleasure just this side of pain, as he captured her ravished lips beneath his mouth.

"Taste yourself." The kiss was slow and deep and drugging. "You taste like sex." An opulent haze settled over her mind. "And sin." He was punctuating his words with nips of his teeth. "A man could get addicted to your taste."

She wanted to ask if he could get addicted to her, but the words clogged in her throat. Hunter's tongue stabbed between her parted lips at the same time he surged into her body. She climaxed the instant he entered her, mind and body shattering so violently that she was only distantly aware of his explosive release.

GILLIAN LAY ON HER BACK, gazing up into the mirror overhead, and decided that while she still thought it tacky, the sight of Hunter's body spread over her was undeniably pleasurable. She skimmed her fingers down his back, over the raised welts left by her short fingernails, and enjoyed the contrast of her pale hand against his dark flesh.

Her other hand traced a line from the strong column of his neck, outward, over his shoulder, down his arm…

"Oh, my God!" The mirror forgotten, she rose to her knees in a flash. "You're bleeding."

Hunter glanced down at the slash on his upper arm. The one he'd completely forgotten about but which, now that she'd drawn his attention to it, had begun to throb.

"It's just a little scratch."

"You've already impressed me with your manliness, Hunter," she countered with a briskness that reminded him she was not all sugar and spice and honeyed sex. Success such as hers did not come to the soft and weak-willed. "So there's no need for the macho-man routine."

Before he could protest her leaving, she was out of the bed. As she marched into the bathroom, Hunter couldn't help noticing that Gillian had the sweetest ass of any woman he'd ever known.

He heard the water running. Then she returned with a damp white washcloth.

She pressed the cloth against the wound, her remarkable eyes narrowing when he involuntarily flinched. "How on earth did this happen?"

"I don't suppose you'd believe me if I said I banged into a shelf of beakers and one broke."

"You don't work with beakers." She frowned as

a poppy-red stain spread across the snowy Egyptian cotton.

"Would you buy the story that I was slicing an onion for a roast beef sandwich and the knife slipped?"

"That's worse than the beaker lie. Obviously you've been stabbed."

"Seen a lot of stab wounds on the concert tour, Sherlock?"

"That's not funny."

"No." Hunter reluctantly had to agree with her there. "I suppose it's not."

"We should call the police."

"The phones are dead," he reminded her.

There was also the little matter of Dylan's sister being police chief of Castle Mountain, and though he'd heard stories about Charity's medal-winning exploits on the LAPD before returning home to take over her late father's job, she wasn't Superwoman. Hunter suspected that in this case, she'd be overmatched.

Even though he'd hated sharing any part of what little personal life he had, Hunter had felt the need to tell the general about his houseguest. Unsurprisingly, he hadn't been assured that Gillian would be protected. Terrorism was an unpredictable thing, the general had reminded Hunter. But he'd do his best.

The problem was, Hunter wasn't all that confident that the man's best would be good enough in this case. If anything happened to Gillian...

He'd have to have another chat with the general, Hunter decided. Tomorrow, before the man left the island and disappeared into that impenetrable military fortress at the Pentagon.

"I wouldn't have thought there were that many muggers on Castle Mountain," Gillian said.

"There aren't."

"Do you know who your attacker was?"

"Nope."

"Then it wasn't personal?"

"Actually, stabbing someone is undoubtedly always personal."

Gillian frowned at his disregard for his own safety. "Does it have something to do with your work?"

"That'd be my guess."

"Should we worry about your attacker showing up here?"

"No." That was the one thing Hunter was absolutely certain about.

At his quick, positive answer, her gaze moved from the blood-brightened cloth to the window. "Is he dead?"

"I suppose so. Unless he somehow managed to sprout wings just before he landed in the sea."

"That seems unlikely."

Hunter was vaguely surprised that she was taking this with such aplomb. Then again, Gillian had been one surprise after another since she'd arrived.

The last of the lingering lust was gone from her eyes. She gave him a long, intelligent, silent look. Then touched the fingertips of the hand that wasn't holding the cloth to his face again, this time to his scarred cheek. Though it took a herculean effort, Hunter did not turn away.

"What happened to you, Hunter?"

"You've already figured that out. Obviously, I was stabbed."

"Not today, but before."

"I was doing research for my project in Bosnia and opened a letter that turned out to be booby-trapped."

"A letter bomb." He watched her slender frame shudder and admired the way she instantly recaptured control of both mind and body. "Your work is that dangerous?"

"Let's just say that if I manage to pull it off, the world could well be a kinder, gentler place."

Frown lines furrowed her smooth brow. "Why would anyone want to kill you for making the world better?"

"Unfortunately, there are a lot of people who don't profit from kinder or gentler and would rather keep the status quo."

"I suppose that makes a certain sort of sad, sick sense." She thought some more. "Do you think this latest attack is related to the one in Bosnia?"

"It could be."

"I see." But, of course she didn't, Hunter acknowledged. Since she had no idea what he was working on. She fell silent again and frowned as she studied his wound. "It might need stitches."

"It'll be fine."

"You're not a doctor."

"Neither are you."

Their gazes met in a silent challenge.

"I hate this," she said finally on a huge huff of breath.

"You don't have to worry. You'll be safe." Somewhere between when he'd first been caught off guard driving home and when his attacker had flown off the cliff, Hunter had made the vow to keep Gillian safe if it was the last thing he did. If it took his final breath on earth.

"I wasn't talking about myself," she said in a rare flare of temper that revealed the passionate woman he'd already discovered her to be. "I hate that you were hurt."

He'd unfastened the metal hook from force of habit when he'd undressed after stumbling with her into the bedroom. At the time, his mind had been as inflamed as his body and he hadn't thought that she might be turned off by the touch of deadened skin against her warm and willing flesh.

He'd tried several prostheses early on in his rehabilitation, but hadn't liked the way they felt like a dead plastic stone at the end of his arm. The hook, while admittedly as ugly as homemade sin, was at least functional. But less-than-conducive to romantic moods.

When he would have pulled his arm away to hide the ruined stump from view, Gillian bent her head. Her cloud of fiery hair tumbled over his forearm as she touched her silken lips to the reddened flesh where his hand had once been. Hunter felt something elemental—as strong and world-shattering as an earthquake—rip through him.

"I got over it." He had to shove the words past the strange boulder suddenly lodged in his throat.

"Physically, perhaps," she allowed. She went on

to press her mouth against each and every one of the white scars that pocked the left side of his chest, her soft butterfly kisses like a benediction.

When she lifted her fingertips to his ruined cheek again and her glistening gaze to his, Hunter was relieved that the explosion had miraculously left both his eyes intact.

"But psychologically? It must have left scars," she insisted softly. "I can't imagine ever getting over the idea someone wanted to kill me."

"Perhaps that's because, despite what you said about your charity work, you still haven't spent the past eight years of your life in war-torn places, hanging out with people who wake up one morning and decide to slaughter all their neighbors."

Those years of research into the dark side of human behavior had given Hunter a different take on good and evil than Gillian's. He wasn't nearly as optimistic. He'd often thought that if there was a God, there was a good chance the guy had given up on his brutal creations.

"Taking a chance on getting killed comes with the territory," he said.

"Perhaps you should change your territory."

"I didn't let your father drive me out of science, Gillian. I'm not going to allow some yahoos with a bit of plastique put a halt to my work."

Since it wasn't germane to the argument, or their situation, he didn't add that he was already looking forward to turning his sights to something less likely to get him blown to smithereens.

"Will you tell me about it?" she asked quietly.

"Exactly what it is you do that has people willing to kill—and die—to stop you?"

"It's classified."

"Just an overview, then," she suggested. "I'm a scientist's daughter," she reminded him unnecessarily. "I understand the importance of keeping research confidential. I'm not asking you to share deep dark government secrets with me, Hunter.

"I just want to know more about what you believe in so strongly that you'd put your own life on the line. But mostly I want to know about you. About your hopes and dreams. The same way you know all about mine."

He could have refused. Hell, he knew he should have refused. But as he found himself drowning in the liquid sea-green depths of her imploring gaze, Hunter feared he was rapidly reaching the point where he'd be unable to refuse this woman anything.

"An overview," he agreed. "After dinner."

She smiled. With her sweet lips and enchanting eyes. "After dinner." She went over to the drawer and selected a scarlet-as-sin satin chemise that skimmed over her breasts like a lover's caress. "Before you make love with me again."

"Again?" he asked with mock surprise as she pulled out a pair of matching panties so skimpy they only covered the essentials. She was a woman made for sexy lingerie, he thought, satisfied that he'd chosen well. "And here I'd thought I'd managed to satisfy you well enough."

"Oh, you have." She tied the crimson ribbons at

her hips. "Splendidly. So well, in fact, that I'm looking forward to you satisfying me again. And again."

Her tone was an enticing blend of honey and smoke, the look she tossed him was so saucy he was almost tempted to pull those scarlet bows loose and drag her back to bed. Hunter stood up, hoping she wouldn't notice that he was gingerly favoring his wounded arm.

"I believe the deal was that you're supposed to be my sex slave."

"Now that you mention it, I do recall something about that game." She went up on her toes and touched her mouth to his. "However, I was thinking that perhaps we might renegotiate the rules."

"Oh?" An electric current surged from her lips to his groin. Would he never get enough of this woman? "What, exactly, are you suggesting?"

"That we take turns playing the subordinate role." Her smile defined vixen.

As humor mixed with lust, Hunter felt his own lips, so unaccustomed to smiling, curve. "For a woman who's traveled the world, you've led a surprisingly sheltered sexual life up until now, Gillian. What makes you believe you're up to the challenge of playing dominatrix?"

She tossed her bright head as she slipped into a matching silk robe that hugged her slender curves and was short enough to make Hunter want to bite her thigh. "Why don't you try me and see?"

He laughed, feeling oddly lighthearted, considering the fact that someone had tried to kill him earlier. "I just may do that."

12

"SO, WHAT YOU DO IS TAKE the political and economic history of a region, plug in sociological factors past and present, along with a genetic profile of the inhabitants, and when you run them through the computer, you can predict how any population is going to respond under any circumstances?"

After nuking a dinner they'd found in the freezer, they'd moved to the library, where Hunter had shared the basics of his research with Gillian. He was not surprised when she immediately grasped his theory. He'd already determined that she was as intelligent as she was beautiful.

"That's it in a nutshell."

She considered it a bit more, sipped her wine, then nodded. "And both the State and Defense Departments are paying you for the study? Isn't that a bit unusual?"

"I suppose." He shrugged. Having spent his life being called everything from a maverick to an eccentric to a madman, Hunter didn't worry much about normalcy. "But they're each taking a different twist on it.

"Defense supposedly wants the data in order to predict wars and know how to best fight them. State, on the other hand, is looking to defuse problems before they blow up. They're also interested in anything that'll give them an edge in negotiating peaceful settlements to skirmishes they can't prevent.''

Hunter didn't mention the feeling he'd been getting that the general, in particular, was seeking something a great deal deadlier from the project.

"I like the State Department's idea best," she decided without hesitation. "Your work should prove a huge help diplomatically."

Her smile was absolutely breathtaking. It literally stole the air from his lungs and did strange, physiologically impossible things to his heart.

"Just think, Hunter, you may actually have hit upon a way to stop wars."

"That's an awfully lofty goal. Even for a man with my ego." But he had admittedly thought of it.

"Goals should be lofty," she declared firmly, making him think of her own not so unreachable goal of playing on the Broadway stage. "Otherwise what would be the point in trying to reach for them?

"Why, without goals, humanity would still be living in caves, and instead of eating Mrs. Adams's excellent pot roast, we'd be forced to go out into the snow and throw sticks and stones at woolly mammoths."

"I believe humanity had moved on to rudimentary weapons at the point in history when people began hunting mammoths."

"Really, Hunter." Her frustrated sigh ruffled her bright bangs. "Must you be so literal?"

"I'm a scientist," he reminded her. "We tend to get mired down in detail."

"You're a social scientist," she reminded him back. "Which means that you're undoubtedly gifted with more imagination than most."

Since he rather liked her thinking he was special, Hunter decided not to point out that any scientist who'd achieved recognition would have the sort of mind that looked beyond the obvious.

"Speaking of imagination," he murmured as he slowly, deliberately put his wineglass down onto the low table in front of them. "What would you say to playing a little fantasy game?"

"What kind of fantasy?"

"I was thinking of something along the lines of an alien invader from outer space."

"I suppose that depends on who gets to play the part of the invader."

"The alien's from a planet in another galaxy that's a parallel universe to Amazonia. Unfortunately, there are no men on the planet, so the very sexually frustrated females have to travel to other planets to fulfill their rampant erotic desires."

Gillian nibbled on her thumbnail as she considered the scenario. "That sounds as if it has possibilities. Do I get to take hostages?"

"Only one."

She sighed dramatically. "Then I suppose I'll have to choose carefully."

"That would be my suggestion."

Her eyes sparkled in the flickering glow of the firelight. Her smile was mischievous and sexy as hell.

"Then I choose you."

As she pressed him back against the dark red leather, Hunter willingly surrendered to the fantasy. To her.

A WINTER SUN WAS STREAMING through the bedroom windows when Gillian awakened. Once again the bed was empty, but she didn't suffer that same feeling of loss this morning because she knew that while Hunter might not yet be prepared to admit it, their relationship had entered a new phase.

It was more than the sex, she considered as she stood beneath the sybaritic shower and luxuriated in the hot water streaming over her body. A body that ached pleasantly after a long, dazzling night of shared fantasies. What was proving even more surprising than Hunter's imagination was her own. She never, in a million years, could have pictured herself being so...well, brazen.

Not that he'd minded. Indeed, for all those long hours, Hunter had willingly surrendered the reins of control to her, and by morning, Gillian had amazed herself with her inventiveness. Hunter, on the other hand, had professed to have no surprise, declaring that he'd known from the first that deep down inside, she was a remarkably passionate woman.

"And he was right," she murmured, feeling more than a little self-satisfied.

But their relationship was more than just dynamite sex. Gillian suspected that Hunter didn't share his work with just anyone, and while he certainly hadn't given her the secret classified computer codes to take

over the world, she also valued the idea that he trusted
her enough to tell her as much as he had.

He'd wanted her from that first night. By the time
they'd made love, he'd let her know that he admired
her. And now he trusted her.

Gillian's lips curved slightly as she ran the sponge
over glowing skin that seemed extraordinarily sensitive since her arrival on Castle Mountain. Surely those
were stepping-stones on the path to love?

She was still smiling as she poured a cup of the
coffee from the carafe already brewed in the kitchen.
He'd also fed the cat, she realized as she viewed the
empty plate and bowl of milk on the floor next to the
box of sleeping kittens. That little evidence of do-
mesticity caused a warm glow to radiate inside her.

She debated tracking him down, worried he'd be
irritated if she intruded on his work, then decided to
take the risk.

"After all," she reasoned as she wound her way
down the hallway toward his office, "Hunter is definitely not a man to do anything he doesn't want to
do. If you're in his way, he'll tell you."

She opened the door and belatedly realized that
Hunter was not alone, which was a surprise, since she
hadn't heard anyone arrive and had been getting accustomed to only the two of them being in the house.

"Good morning." Hunter greeted her with a smile,
but she could detect little seeds of worry in his eyes.

"Good morning. I'm sorry, I didn't mean to interrupt."

She was also vastly grateful that she'd chosen to
put a long black silk robe over a nightgown of mid-

night lace that revealed more than it covered. She wasn't exactly dressed for company, but at least she was fairly decent.

"Don't worry about it. We were just finishing up." He rose. "This is Dylan Prescott," he said, introducing her to the man who'd also stood up. "He established the brain factory. Dylan, this is—"

"Gillian Cassidy." The man was handsome in a rakish, boyish way. His grin, which touched his intelligent eyes, was rich and warm, and although Gillian was certain that it had undoubtedly coaxed its share of women into sharing sexual favors, it didn't move her nearly as much as a half smile from Hunter could. "I'm a huge fan."

"What a nice thing to say."

"It's the truth," he said easily. "My wife's a fan, too. In fact, she keeps duplicates of all your CDs in her car."

"Oh, I do like to hear that." Feeling more at ease than when she'd first opened the door and found the stranger with Hunter, Gillian smiled.

"I also have instructions to invite you to dinner," he revealed. "Perhaps Hunter would be willing to share you long enough for the four of us to attend Winterfest together this weekend. It's the island's annual festival."

"Gillian won't be staying on the island that long," Hunter said quickly, brusquely, before Gillian could respond.

"I see." Dylan glanced over at Hunter, then returned his attention to Gillian. "Perhaps next time you visit," he suggested, changing gears smoothly.

The tension in the room was palpable, like the precipitous drop of the barometer before a violent storm. Gillian sensed an unspoken message flash between the two men and suspected that somehow it involved her.

"I'd like that," she agreed faintly.

"Didn't you say something about needing to get back to your own work?" Hunter asked Dylan. Once again his attitude was brusque, bordering on rude.

"That's right, I did," Dylan responded on cue.

Gillian guessed that the founder of any research lab where Hunter would work would undoubtedly be brilliant. That didn't make him a good actor. His tone and behavior were both decidedly forced.

"Gillian, it's been a pleasure meeting you." That, at least, seemed genuine. Dylan took her hand in both of his. His eyes, as they met hers, seemed to be filled with sympathy.

She murmured a similar statement as Hunter practically dragged the scientist away.

HUNTER WAS NOT SURPRISED to find Gillian waiting for him when he returned from seeing Dylan out of the house.

"You weren't serious, were you?" she asked. "About me leaving?"

"Actually, I was." Because Hunter dreaded the wounded-puppy look he feared he'd see in her eyes, he began shuffling through some computer printouts on his desk. "You knew, when you first arrived, that I wasn't interested in a permanent relationship, Gillian."

"You made that point perfectly clear." Her tone was icy, but Hunter easily heard the heat lurking beneath it and once again considered that Gillian was definitely a woman of contrasts. "You brought me here to have sex with you for thirty nights. In case you've been too wrapped up in your work to look at a calendar, that time isn't nearly up."

He shrugged, still keeping his attention on the pages of data. "Perhaps the game has worn a little thin." Although it was one of the most difficult things he'd ever done, he made himself look her directly in the eyes. "Perhaps I've grown tired of you."

Hunter heard her sharp intake of breath and hated himself as he watched the color drain from her cheeks, leaving her looking as fragile and transparent as crystal. But then, as he watched with fascination and admiration, the wounded wraith turned into the female warrior she'd played last night with such stimulating perfection.

"I don't believe you." Hectic red battle flags waved in her cheeks. Her eyes glistened. Hunter wondered whether the tears she was refusing to shed were born of pain or anger. "But it doesn't matter, because a deal's a deal, Hunter. In case you've overlooked the impetus for all this, I'm here because my father cheated you so horribly."

Determined to get her out of the house and off the island, where she'd be safe, Hunter wasn't about to admit that they'd moved far beyond that.

"You profess to be a man of honor," she reminded him firmly. "Men of honor keep their word. And our deal was for thirty days."

"Nights," he corrected her on a mild murmur.

"Thirty nights," she agreed with a toss of her fiery head, which, as important as this conversation was, had him recalling how it had felt like burning silk against his thighs last night. "So, like it or not, Hunter St. John, you're stuck with me until the time's up. If you're truly bored, and you don't want to make love—have sex," she corrected quickly when his eyes narrowed, "fine."

She folded her arms across the front of the black silk robe. "Having spent twenty-five years sleeping alone, I won't die of loneliness. However, wherever you spend those nights, or with whom, I'm not leaving."

If it wasn't so serious, if he wasn't so worried about her, if he didn't want to get her off the island, Hunter would have almost been amused by the way she held her ground.

He shook his head and tried to reassure himself that as long as no one could reach Castle Mountain due to the storm, she should be safe.

"George was right. You're not easily tamed."

She was also not one to hold a grudge. She smiled, a slow, siren's smile that he feared would linger in his memory and still excite him when he was in his nineties and living in some retirement home for mad scientists.

"Perhaps," she suggested, with a bold-as-brass look as she untied the black silk sash at her waist, "you just need to work a little harder at it."

She shrugged the robe off her shoulders and walked toward him, letting it slide to the floor. The gown she was wearing beneath it was created of delicate black lace. The way it was cut high on the sides, all the way up to her hips, displayed her gorgeous, wrap-around legs. As she moved closer, the shifting lace offered tantalizing glimpses of perfumed and powdered female flesh.

''Tell me again,'' she suggested as she twined her arms around his neck.

''Tell you what?'' She was rubbing against him, like a sleek, sensuous cat.

''How much I bore you.'' She slid down his body, her hands clever, her touch confident. ''How much you don't want me.'' Hunter drew in a breath as she deftly dispatched the five metal buttons on his jeans.

''Tell me that you don't want me to do this.'' Her long, slim, talented pianist's fingers encircled his aching shaft. ''Or this.'' His body tensed with anticipation as she stroked its length; his self-control was hanging by a single ragged thread.

''And, of course, I know how you've grown so weary of me doing this.'' When she took him in her mouth, fully, deeply, wetly, the thread snapped.

MUCH, MUCH LATER, GILLIAN lifted her head and grinned down at Hunter. They'd ended up on the rug, Hunter on his back, Gillian on top of him, her legs splayed over his hips, their clothes scattered. She'd thought she'd heard the sound of lace ripping, but caught up in her own seduction efforts, she hadn't cared.

''Well?'' she asked.

''You're a saucy wench, I'll give you that,'' he

allowed as he ran a hand down the cooling flesh of her back.

"I am, aren't I?" She smiled, pleased for them both.

"Unfortunately, you may have overlooked one important thing."

"What's that?"

"If you kill me before the thirty days are up, you'll have to leave early."

"Don't worry, Hunter." She brushed her lips over his. "I promise to be gentle with you from now on."

She felt his mouth curve beneath hers. "Thank you, Gillian. I'm extremely grateful."

"How grateful?"

"It's difficult to put into words." He rolled them over in a swift, lithe move that put him on top. "Perhaps I should demonstrate, instead."

It was Hunter who was gentle. This time their lovemaking was different. His kisses were as soft as snowflakes, as warm and intoxicating as mulled wine. His hands were slow and patient and knowing, touching her in all the places he'd discovered she loved to be touched. He savored, tenderly, lingeringly.

Outside, the blizzard continued to rage. Inside, shimmering jewel-toned rainbows filled Gillian's head and ripples of delight rode in her veins, spinning like a kaleidoscope when she climaxed.

"You're crying." He touched a fingertip to the tear that had accompanied her release.

"Only because it was so..." She'd already discovered that sex with Hunter could be thrilling. But she hadn't expected it to be so exquisitely beautiful. "Amazing."

He laughed, that rough, slightly rusty sound that suggested it was not something he did often. "It's us." He brushed some damp curls away from her face. "We're amazing together, Gillian. A perfect match, just as I'd suspected."

Although Gillian understood that Hunter was still talking about sex, she vowed that before her time on Castle Mountain had come to an end, he'd realize that they were a perfect match in every way.

Over the next few days, as the storm waned, Gillian held her breath, half expecting Hunter to once again attempt to send her away. But he didn't.

They no longer spent their days apart. Gillian's sexuality blossomed, like a late summer rose opening to the sun. Trusting Hunter implicitly, there was nothing she would not do, no suggestion or request she would say no to. In return, Hunter marveled at her sexual imagination, not realizing, or perhaps not acknowledging, Gillian had thought on more than one occasion, that love was driving everything she did.

Since even they could not make love all the time, they began to share far more than just their bodies. They spent hours together in the library, Gillian at the piano, Hunter lounging on the leather sofa, his eyes closed, seeming to absorb the music. In the past she'd always preferred privacy when she was composing, but soon discovered that having Hunter in the room stimulated her creativity and raised the emotionalism of her work to new heights.

Because his work was so highly classified, Gillian

couldn't help with his research. But she did proofread two articles he'd agreed to write for scientific journals, both which she declared brilliant. She also began spending the morning hours in his office, curled up with a book while he tapped away on the computer.

And when Mrs. Adams's doctor, upon reexamination, found a hairline fracture in the housekeeper's ankle, delaying her return to the house, Gillian discovered culinary talents that surprised her even more than her newfound sexuality.

She enjoyed cooking for Hunter, an enjoyment that increased when he began to spend evenings puttering around in the kitchen with her. Since more often than not they tended to get sidetracked during preparation, they quickly learned to stick to dishes that could be heated up later. After other hungers had been satisfied.

"Tell me about your parents," she asked one night, while they were eating a late supper in bed. Across the room the fire crackled; outside the glass wall a full moon floated in a clear winter sky studded with white stars.

They'd begun discussing more personal aspects of their lives, as well, and while Hunter had proved more reticent than she, Gillian continued to delve for more information about this man she loved.

"They were both a lot like your father. Brilliant and horrendously egocentric." He scooped up a forkful of baked spaghetti. "My father was David St. John."

"The British physicist." A man whose name was

legendary in the scientific community. Even more famous than her father's.

"That's him. My mother was Isabel Montgomery. She was an American biochemist, who was less known than my father at the time but no less intelligent and perhaps even more ambitious. Her entire life focused around her work."

He took a bite of the now-cold spaghetti, frowning as he chewed. "They divorced before I was two, so I can't remember them together as a couple, but from what each of them said individually about the other, I'd guess that their marriage was pretty horrific.

"I spent some time bouncing back and forth between them, which meant mostly spending my days with household staff. When I was five, my mother was offered a research grant to study the medicinal possibilities of plants in the rain forest. Promising to be back before I knew it, she left me with my maternal grandmother."

The no-nonsense New York widow of a wealthy industrialist who'd cornered the world market on copper, Gillian remembered reading in that *Newsweek* article.

"A year led to two, then five. Then more. The summer I turned fifteen she died of some tropical fever."

Gillian placed a hand on his arm. "I'm sorry."

Hunter shrugged. "I didn't spend much time grieving for her. It was impossible to miss something—or someone—you never had. Coincidentally, my father died that same winter, in a car crash in Monaco."

"Leaving you an orphan."

His rough answering laugh held neither humor nor

bitterness. "It wasn't nearly as Dickensian as you make it sound. By the time he drove his sports car off that cliff, I doubt if I could have picked him out in a lineup. It'd been years since I'd seen him in anything but newspaper articles or news clips."

"That's even sadder."

"I suppose it depends on your viewpoint." Hunter shrugged. "When I first arrived at my grandmother's Park Avenue apartment, where I stayed a day before being shipped back to boarding school, she informed me that the only reason I existed was because her daughter—and there was no love lost between the two of them, believe me—had wanted to perpetuate her own genes. I suspect that was my father's motive, as well."

"I can understand that. My father always regretted not having a son to keep his gene pool alive."

"Yet more proof that your father is a fool." He gave her a studied look.

Since he'd been opening up to her more with each passing day, Gillian decided to take a chance. "I suppose that growing up without close family ties is another thing we have in common," she said carefully.

His face closed up. "I suppose so."

She watched the shutters slamming shut over his eyes. Damn. Gillian understood all too well why Hunter didn't trust relationships, but it was still frustrating, and a bit daunting, when he turned so distant on her.

Recognizing the brick wall of resistance, she decided to sidestep around it. For now.

"Tomorrow's Saturday."

"So?"

"Didn't Dylan Prescott say something about a winter carnival this weekend?"

"I believe he may have mentioned it."

She took a deep breath, then went for broke. "I thought we might go."

"To Winterfest?"

He looked as if she'd suggested taking a rocket to Mars. Actually, Gillian thought, there was a very good chance that he'd find that suggestion more reasonable.

"I've never been to a winter carnival," she said. There had, of course, been winter festivals in the Alps, but the nuns, determined to protect the chastity of their charges, and understanding that might be difficult when music was playing, people were dancing and wine and beer were flowing, had never let the girls attend.

"Neither have I."

"All the more reason to go."

Hunter considered that argument as he finished the spaghetti. "I have no idea what one even does at such an event."

"Well—" she shrugged and offered him her sweetest smile "—I suppose attending is a good way to find out. Surely you've wondered."

He thought about that for a moment. "No." He placed the empty earthenware bowl onto the black lacquered table beside the bed. "I haven't."

Gillian let out a frustrated breath. "And here I thought you possessed scientific curiosity. Why don't you try thinking of it as mingling with the natives?"

His eyes swept over her again. "It means that much to you?"

"Yes." She had no real idea why, but it did.

A muscle moved in his scarred jaw. He didn't answer for another long moment.

"If I do this for you, I'll want something in return."

"That's only fair." She had a very good idea of what sort of quid pro quo he was referring to and knew that there was nothing he'd suggest she'd consider a sacrifice.

"We won't stay long."

"Just long enough to get the flavor of the event," she agreed.

He nodded. Slowly. And still a bit reluctantly. "All right. We'll go."

His willingness to leave his stunning glass-and-cedar fortress caused joy to sing in Gillian's veins. She flung her arms around his neck.

"Thank you, Hunter. I promise you'll have a wonderful time."

He pushed her back against the pillows. "Believe me, Gillian, I intend to."

When she'd first arrived on Castle Mountain, Gillian would have believed Hunter's words to be a threat. Now, as she kissed him back, wildly, wonderfully, she took them as a promise.

13

"OH, IT'S JUST LIKE the Emerald City, but white," Gillian breathed as she and Hunter arrived in the small New England town that had given the Maine island its name.

The trees lining the brick sidewalks of Main Street had been sprayed with water, which had frozen to a crystalline brilliance. Fairy lights twinkled in the winter-bare branches. A towering ice castle claimed the town square, gleaming in the spotlights focused on it. More tiny white lights illuminated the tall, icy turrets.

"Now all we need are some munchkins," he said dryly.

"Too kinky," she responded as she spotted an entire group of ice sculptures created by Castle Mountain residents.

"You promised me anything."

"I lied." She stared up at the huge ice moose and wondered if the real thing could possibly be so large. "So sue me."

"I'd rather kiss you." And he did. Lightly, tenderly, a mere whispered promise of a kiss that nevertheless had her toes curling in her boots.

A sturdy draft horse approached, its harness lit up with more white lights, huge hoofs clip-clopping.

"New idea," Hunter said. He took hold of her mittened hand. "I'll bet you've never made love in a sleigh."

"Of course not!" But the idea, along with the wicked glint in his sexy eyes, caused a flush to rise in her cheeks. "And I've no intention of trying. If we didn't freeze to death, we'd undoubtedly get arrested."

He shook his head. "It's bad enough that you're admitting you lied when you told me you'd do anything," he said with a deep, feigned sigh. "I suppose next you're going to forget that you promised me that if we came to Winterfest, you'd make certain I had a wonderful time."

"I may have changed a bit since I first came to Castle Mountain—"

"Blossomed."

"What?"

"You haven't really changed, Gillian. Not really. The person you are tonight is the same woman you've always been, deep down inside. What's happened is that the freedom to act on those inner impulses you've always put into your music has made you blossom into a gorgeous, exciting sexual adventuress."

It was true. Even so, Gillian quickly looked around to make certain that no passing festival-goer had heard his murmured comment.

"You may have a point. So far as it goes." She noticed that he'd deftly left out any reference to love. "But while I'm willing to explore my sensual side at home, I'm not adventurous enough to make love in public.'' He might be hesitant to say the word, but she was weary of trying to conceal her true feelings.

''So, it was a dandy festival, can we leave now?''

She laughed. One of the things that had surprised her about these past days with Hunter was that their relationship also included an easy humor that, in the beginning, she wouldn't have thought possible.

''I would have thought, that being a scientist, you should have learned patience.''

''I thought I was remarkably patient with you when you first arrived. Do you have any idea how many showers I took trying to give you time to adjust to your situation?''

''You also wanted me to spend that time thinking about you. About how it would be when we went to bed together. What you wanted,'' she accused lightly, ''was to make me crazy with wanting.''

''That, too,'' he agreed. ''So, did it work?''

''If you need any more proof, Hunter, I'd say that your observation skills need a lot of work.''

It was his turn to laugh as he led her over to where the sleigh had stopped beside a towering ice structure that reminded Gillian of Sleeping Beauty's castle. Which in turn made her think of how, in a way, she'd been sleeping until Hunter had awakened her to the total, sensual woman she could be.

''Wrong movie,'' she murmured minutes later as she snuggled beneath a pile of blankets in the back of the sleigh. Harness bells jingled merrily, metal runners crunched against the snow, stars glistened overhead.

''Hmm?'' When he touched his lips to the top of

her head, as impossible as it was, Gillian imagined she felt the heat of the kiss through the barrier of her red wool ski cap.

"Main Street may resemble Oz in winter, but this is right out of *Dr. Zhivago*." There may have been more romantic ways to spend a December evening, but Gillian couldn't think of one.

He pulled her closer, put his gloved fingers on her chin and tilted her face up to his. "We'll have a happier ending."

Gillian didn't want to talk about endings. Not when the waning moon overhead signaled that they'd passed the halfway point in their agreed-upon time together.

She didn't answer, but instead closed the distance between them, kissing Hunter with a rush of feeling that brought tears to her eyes.

While the fantasy of making love in the back of a sleigh was admittedly tempting, Gillian was relieved when Hunter seemed satisfied with long, slow, hot kisses that made her forget the temperature had dropped below freezing.

She was snuggled up against him, able to feel his thickening erection even through the layers of thick outdoor clothing between them. When she pressed her palm against the bulge in his jeans, he groaned.

"Wench," he murmured in her ear, so as not to be heard by the driver, who had his wool watch cap pulled down low over his ears. "You realize, of course, that we're not playing alien dominatrix tonight. I could punish you for that." As if to underscore his silky threat, he pushed the hood of her parka back and bit her earlobe. Gently, but enough to cause a tingle of anticipation.

"You wouldn't dare." Her chin was up, her eyes flashed confidence. He might not be willing to admit he loved her, but neither would he humiliate or embarrass her. "Not in public. Not in front of all these people who know you."

Gillian's words were a dare. And they both knew it. His responding smile was slow, and wonderfully wicked. "Want to bet?"

An instant later, she felt a deep throbbing between her legs. "Hunter!"

"Yes, Gillian?" he asked with feigned innocence. Even as he pulled a bit away from her, severing physical contact, the throbbing deepened, stimulating already overly sensitive nerve endings.

It was the bikini panties, she realized. The ones he'd given her earlier this evening and asked her to wear tonight. But how could that be possible? Hadn't she held them up to the light, noticing that they were so sheer she could see her hand behind the nearly transparent black silk?

"What... Oh, my God," she moaned, writhing, just a bit beneath the blankets as she felt the familiar sexual tension coiling inside her.

Her senses swam. Her mind was shutting down, her thoughts drifting away, allowing her to concentrate only on the magnificent sensations flowing through her.

She closed her eyes tight, imagining that she was flying up to the star-spangled sky, soaring through the

Milky Way, soaring, wheeling, touching the glittering blue-white tips of the stars.

Though he hadn't touched her, the orgasm swept over her like a wave. No longer flying, she came crashing down, as if into the sea, and clung to him, her arms twined tightly around his neck, as she might cling onto a piece of driftwood to keep from drowning. Not in the icy Atlantic, but in the dangerous, swirling depths of her own emotions.

"How on earth did you do that?"

Her cheek was pressed against the front of his jacket, muffling her words. But he heard her nevertheless.

"You'd be amazed at what technology is capable of these days."

"I imagine so. But surely I would have felt something different." He must have hypnotized her. Or perhaps, she thought fancifully, on this one magical night, Hunter could have become a wizard and cast a spell upon her. "And there aren't any wires connecting me to any power source."

"Wires are passé. I used radio waves with a receiver that's not much thicker than a human hair, which kept you from feeling it. The concept isn't really that complicated. The average computer nerd could probably make one with stuff from Radio Shack."

"I doubt if the average computer nerd would even think of such a thing."

"You may have a point."

He reached into his jacket pocket and took out a small black box about the size of the matchboxes that her mother had once collected from famous restaurants around the world. When he flicked a small switch with his gloved hand, the renewed humming against her still tingling body caused her to gasp.

"Hunter! Are you saying you've created radio controlled underwear?"

Damn. She closed her eyes and cringed with embarrassment as she realized that her surprise had made her speak loudly enough that the driver might have actually been able to hear her over the jingling of the sleigh bells. But he didn't turn his head, and the pace of the horse didn't change, so she desperately hoped that perhaps he hadn't been listening all that closely.

"I was considering making a model boat. But it's too cold to spend much time outdoors this time of year, it would undoubtedly crash on the rocks, anyway, and this seemed like a lot more fun. Want to test the limits?"

He flicked the knob to high and nearly had her coming on the spot.

"Stop that!" she hissed. "How do you know you won't electrocute me?"

"I wouldn't do that." He turned the knob to off again. "Besides, you're perfectly safe. So long as it doesn't rain."

Gillian tilted her head and looked at him. "If keeping dry is necessary to prevent electrocution," she said, referring to the moisture gathering between her thighs, "I'm in danger of looking like the bride of Frankenstein any minute."

He chuckled about that, seeming to enjoy himself immensely. "Wait until you see the matching bra.

That's a little trickier. I couldn't quite get it finished before we left, but perhaps we could give it a trial run when we get home.''

The idea of Hunter being able to stimulate her in such a way, whenever he wanted, without even touching her, definitely tipped the power in their relationship back toward him.

''For a man who thinks light-years into the future, there are times, and this is one of them, when you're definitely a throwback to the eighteenth or nineteenth century. Maybe even medieval times. No, even that's not far back enough. How about the Stone Age?''

''Are you calling me Cro-Magnon man?''

''If the club fits,'' she murmured dryly. ''This is undoubtedly the most politically incorrect invention you've ever come up with.''

But outrageously exciting. Gillian tried to tell herself that it was only the cold that had caused her nipples to harden like gemstones, but she knew that it was the erotic thought of Hunter's specially created bra vibrating against her tender breasts.

''You may be right. But I'll bet it's the most fun.''

She couldn't argue that. ''I suppose,'' she said, ''that depends on whether I also end up picking up signals from automatic garage door openers all over town.''

He laughed, sounding, she thought, entirely pleased with himself. ''I suppose that could add an unexpected dimension to the game. But I chose a low-frequency band. You shouldn't have to worry.''

''Well, that's something. You didn't happen to sew

any of those fiber optics into those briefs you're wearing, did you?"

"Not yet. But if you insist, I could give it the old college try."

"I insist."

His smile was slow, seductive, and she suspected he'd already expected this outcome. "I'll say this for you, Gillian. You're definitely exceeding expectations." He bent his head and brushed his mouth against hers, nibbling at her bottom lip. "I've half a mind to keep you."

"Neanderthal," she muttered, even as she had to fight her own desire to suggest that he do precisely that.

They came to the end of the ride, and driver and horse pulled to a stop. Gillian was pleased and more than a little relieved when she discovered that her legs were steadier than they'd felt only minutes earlier. She was also pleased when Hunter kept his gloved fingers off the control device.

But she remained aware of it in his jacket pocket, and the knowledge that he could stimulate her anywhere, at any time, as he wished and at his will, right here in public in front of what appeared to be all the residents of the island, heightened her senses until she felt a bit like a downed electrical wire, amazed that she wasn't throwing off sparks.

The rest of the evening passed in a romantic blur. Hunter's appearance at the festival earned a few curious glances from some of Castle Mountain's residents, but Gillian suspected that was as much due to surprise at seeing the island's famous recluse out in public as it was to his scarred physical appearance.

They ate like greedy children, moving from booth to booth, working their way through a plethora of tasty treats: maple sugar cookies, spiced apple cider, caramel corn, creamy dark fudge studded with hazelnuts and divinity that looked like bits of fluffy white clouds and tasted like heaven. Huge outdoor radiant heaters had been set up to warm the crowds and a bonfire blazed at the edge of the ice skating pond.

It had taken a bit more coaxing, but Gillian had gotten Hunter into a pair of rented black hockey skates, and while they certainly weren't going to win any medals for ice dancing anytime soon, they'd managed to make several turns around the snow-bordered pond without falling down.

She heard a voice call Hunter's name. When they turned back toward the shore, Gillian was pleased to see Dylan skating toward her with another man and two women.

"How great you managed to stay for our little celebration, after all," he said, skidding to a stop in front of her with a little spray of shaved ice. His grin was warm as the roasted chestnuts Gillian had sampled earlier.

"I'm having a wonderful time," she said.

He went on to introduce her to the people with him: his wife, Julianna, a science fiction author; his brother-in-law, Bram Starbuck, an astrophysicist also working at the brain factory; and his sister, Charity, who, Gillian learned, had once served on the LAPD force before returning to Castle Mountain to take over her late father's position as chief of police.

Charity welcomed Gillian with a warmth that echoed her brother's, while Julianna, who reminded Gillian of a young Jackie Kennedy, was more reserved, but friendly. As was Bram Starbuck. All immediately declared themselves fans.

. "It's so wonderful to see you out and about, Hunter." Charity glided a little forward on her figure skates. "It's been much too long."

"I've been tied up in my work."

"So Dylan tells me. Still, you know what they say about all work and no play. Besides, your friends miss you." She hugged him with obvious affection.

Gillian felt a little prick of jealousy as she watched Hunter hug the other woman back. When she belatedly noticed that Charity was pregnant beneath the thick down parka, jealousy was replaced by a sharp, unbidden stab of what felt uncomfortably like envy.

"How are you?" Charity asked Hunter as she backed away. Gillian watched her husband reach out and take a protective hold of her arm to balance her on the glassy surface. "Really?"

"Just fine," he responded mildly. "How are things in the law enforcement business?"

"Oh, you know. The usual." She shrugged and glanced over at Gillian. "Castle Mountain isn't exactly the crime capital of the world. Mostly we get calls about barking dogs, snowplows blocking driveways, that sort of thing...."

"Though we did have a little excitement yesterday.'' She turned her gaze back toward Hunter. ''A body washed up on the rocks below the lighthouse.''

''Really?'' he responded with studied casualness. ''I suppose it was a fisherman washed overboard during the squall.''

''That's undoubtedly the case,'' she agreed, equally as mildly. ''Funny thing, though. He wasn't a local.''

Hunter shrugged. ''It's a big ocean. I suppose he could have washed up from the mainland.''

''Yes.'' Gillian watched the woman's perceptive blue eyes search his inscrutable face. ''That seems to be the case. Unfortunately, he didn't have any ID on him, which, since the lighthouse is government property, means the feds are getting involved.''

With that unsettling statement hanging on the frosty night air, she turned toward Gillian. ''Did I hear that you've recently ended a world tour?''

If Castle Mountain's police chief did know about Hunter's encounter with the mystery drowning victim, she didn't seem inclined to discuss the matter in public.

Grateful for the change in subject, Gillian began sharing a few of the more colorful moments of her tour to the amusement of these people who were so obviously fond of Hunter. But she was all too aware of him standing silently beside her, lost in his own thoughts and, she felt, a great deal more tense than he had been when they'd first taken to the ice.

''THANK YOU,'' GILLIAN murmured later as they drove back through the darkened woods to the house.

Hunter glanced over at her. ''For what?''

"For the most wonderful night of my life. I can't remember when I've had a better time."

His grin was a slash of white in the blackness surrounding them. "And just think, the night's still young."

She grinned back, sensual anticipation humming in her veins. Then the concern that had been niggling at her mind since meeting Charity returned.

"Charity knew, didn't she? About you being attacked."

"Yeah. Since it's difficult for her to keep things off the record, I didn't want to bring her into it unless it became absolutely necessary. But Castle Mountain is not only her jurisdiction, but the home she grew up in, and I suppose it's only fair that she be warned. I suspect Dylan told her just enough to let her know that she's dealing with something a lot more complicated than the usual Saturday night drunk-and-disorderly call from the Stewed Clam."

"Will it be a problem? Having federal agents investigating your attack?"

"Not really. Once the phones are back in service, I'll just have to make a few calls to Washington to keep them off our backs. Since I don't really have any information that could prove helpful."

"When do you think the phones might be working again?" Enjoying being cut off from the outside world for this stolen, magical time with Hunter, Gillian wasn't all that eager for service to be resumed.

"It's hard to say. The village usually gets service before the more remote places like the lab."

"Or your house."

"Yeah."

"Mrs. Adams said the sea is calm enough for Ben to begin his mail boat crossings tomorrow." She'd run into the housekeeper being pushed in a wheelchair by her husband at the pie-judging booth where, unsurprisingly, Mildred Adams had won the blue ribbon for her blueberry buckle.

"I heard her."

"Does that mean the investigators might show up at the house before you can have them called off?"

For the first time in as long as he could remember, Hunter had no desire to think about the future. "Let's worry about that tomorrow, okay?"

"Okay." She smiled that dazzling, sock-a-guy-in-the-groin smile that had managed to knock him out every time he watched her video. "Would it be possible to pull over safely?"

The out-of-the-blue question surprised him. Until Hunter remembered all the cider she'd drunk. On top of the cold...

"Sure. I can find a spot. If you really need to."

"Oh, I really, really do."

"No problem." The layers of warm clothing might be, though, he considered.

He managed to find a gravel turnout that had obviously been plowed recently, pulled off the road and cut the engine. "The snow's pretty deep," he warned. "I'd better get out and open your door and—"

"That's not necessary." She caught hold of his arm. The overhead light had come on when he'd opened the driver's door, revealing the seductive gleam in her eyes. "You know, of course, that I spent my teenage years in the protective custody of nuns."

"I seem to recall George mentioning that."

"Switzerland is a very pretty country. But imprisoned as I was in that convent school, I've never had the opportunity to make love in the back seat of a car." Smiling, she unfastened her seat belt, then unzipped the parka. "It's always been one of my fantasies."

She shrugged out of the jacket, tossed it into the back seat and pulled the scarlet cashmere sweater over her head, revealing absolutely nothing underneath.

Hunter swallowed. He could have been looking at her for the first time. Her breasts shone like marble in the white moonlight, but he knew that they were much softer. And a great deal warmer.

"I thought you were the one who was worried about freezing to death."

"That was then." She began wiggling out of her jeans. "This is now."

Hunter swore, wondering yet again which of them was more crazy and deciding that they both were. Crazy with lust.

He helped her with her jeans, ripping them down past her knees, where they came to a stop when he reached her boots. At the same time her hands were busy on his jacket. Buttons flew from the front of his thick flannel shirt, hitting with little pings against the dashboard before dropping onto the rubber floormats.

"Thank God you're not wearing those damn button-fly jeans," she said as she yanked the zipper down and took him into her smooth and dangerous hands.

"I'll burn every last pair tomorrow," he promised as he tore away the scanty bit of silk between her thighs, effectively destroying his latest invention.

They never made it to the back seat. Instead, he took her hard and fast on the reclining passenger seat, ramming into her like a wild man as her fingers dug into his bare buttocks and her hips bucked.

The shared orgasm shuddered through them, stronger than he'd ever experienced and seemingly endless. Hunter drank in her hoarse cries of completion and resisted, just barely, howling like a triumphant timber wolf.

Their cooling bodies were moist and slick. Still bracing himself on his arms, Hunter buried his face against her neck and considered how humiliating it would be if they had to call 911 because he was having a heart attack and Charity found him with his pants down around his ankles, like some teenager caught by a patrolling cop at lover's lane.

He felt as if the climax had sucked all the air out of his lungs. He obviously wasn't alone in that regard since beneath him, Gillian was panting. Outside the steamed-up windows, a snowy owl hooted in the moon-spangled darkness.

"That was," she murmured finally, "even better than the fantasy."

"We never got to the back seat," he pointed out as he dragged himself back to his own seat and tried to muster up the strength to pull up his briefs and jeans.

She'd located the panties, realized they were ruined, shrugged, then began wiggling her jeans up in a way that, if he wasn't still on the verge of death, would have made Hunter want to do it all again.

"Next time," she suggested, flashing him a smile as she climbed up on her knees and reached over the back of the seat for her parka.

"Next time," he agreed, wondering vaguely if his life insurance was paid up. Deciding that it didn't really matter, since he didn't have any heirs and couldn't think of a better way to go, Hunter set about getting dressed.

While time had seemed suspended, the dashboard clock revealed that less than ten minutes had passed since she'd asked him to pull over. And probably half of those, Hunter thought, had been spent dealing with the heavy winter outerwear. Still, what it lacked in length had been made up for in intensity.

"Hunter?"

"Hmm?"

The sky overhead was still clear, resembling the dome of a planetarium. There were no new storms on the horizon. Hunter's mind drifted to the federal agents who'd undoubtedly be arriving on the island tomorrow. He could handle them. It was whoever else might show up that had him more concerned. Not for himself. But for Gillian.

"I love you."

Caught unaware, he stiffened.

"Don't."

She folded her arms. "Too late."

He could feel her looking at him, but kept gazing

straight ahead, at the windshield. It was late at night, the narrow, twisting road was icy, only a fool would let his attention wander from his driving.

And only a coward would refuse to meet his lover's soft, imploring gaze.

A million thoughts were spinning through his mind, most of them centered around why Gillian loving him was impossible. He was not a man who lied, not even to himself. Most particularly to himself.

Hunter knew that he was scarred. Outside and inside. He also knew that while he could tell you, better than most, why a group of indigenous people might behave in any given way, he had no idea how to be anyone's husband. Or father.

That thought sent fingers of icy fear skimming up his spine. He reminded himself that he'd always taken precautions, never allowed himself to get so aroused that he'd forget protection.

Until tonight.

"If anything happens…" He could explain genetic profiling to an international gathering of the planet's greatest minds, but he couldn't find the words to say what he needed to say to this woman. "After tonight…"

"Something did happen. I just told you that I loved you."

"You're confusing sex with love. Which isn't that surprising. After all, you were a virgin before I forced you to come here—"

"I was a virgin by choice. I'm also an adult, Hunter. You didn't force me to do anything. Perhaps your little blackmail scheme was the impetus for me coming to the island in the first place, but once I arrived at your house, I was a willing participant in everything. Including tonight.''

''If you get pregnant, I'll want to know.'' He still wasn't looking at her.

''Really?'' He heard her shift in her seat and knew that she'd turned toward him. ''Why? Would you offer to make an honest woman of me?''

''You're already an honest woman.'' Too damn honest for her own good.

''I told you I was,'' she reminded him. ''What would you do, Hunter? If you found out I was carrying your child?''

''I'd want to be involved.''

''Involved. That's an interesting, albeit remote way of putting it. Are you saying you'd change diapers, walk the floor, drive our son to Little League games?''

''I don't know, dammit!'' He shot a short, frustrated glance at her. ''I've never given it any thought before tonight.''

''Really?'' The irritated edge to her voice was gone, replaced by genuine curiosity. ''You've never fantasized about having children?''

''Never.''

''Why not?''

''How the hell should I know?'' He raked a frustrated hand through his hair and considered pulling off the road and making love again to her just to get her off this topic.

He could feel her long, steady look. ''I think that's the saddest thing I've ever heard.''

"Then you've been too sheltered. Because believe me, baby, there are a helluva lot sadder things in the world than not having to put up with a miniature of me."

The silence spun out in the dark confines of the Suburban as she considered that declaration. "You know," she said finally, slowly, "for a supposedly brilliant man, you can really be an idiot."

There was no way he could disagree with that.

"Will you tell me?" he pressed. "If you get pregnant?"

He heard her shimmering sigh and wondered how such a soft, resigned sound could tug so many unwanted emotional chords. "I'll tell you."

Hunter wondered why her answer, which he'd insisted on, failed to give him any satisfaction. He tried to think of something to say, something that would make things right, to put them back the way they'd been when he'd been holding her during the sleigh ride. When he'd kissed her beneath a canopy of brilliant stars and wished he possessed the power to stop the world from spinning.

He might be an idiot when it came to relationships, but even Hunter knew that none of the words that came to mind—pat, easy, safe phrases he was used to saying to women—fit this occasion.

So, miserable coward that he was, he took the easy way out and said nothing.

14

GILLIAN WAS NOT ALL that surprised when Hunter didn't speak to her the rest of the way back to the house. She even understood why he might choose to spend the night locked away in his office rather than joining her in the huge, too lonely bed. It was more than a little obvious that no one had ever loved him before. It would just take some time for him to get used to the idea. Gillian was a patient woman. Since she knew, deep down inside, that she wasn't alone in her feelings, she was prepared to wait.

After a restless, mostly sleepless night, she was still giving herself that little pep talk the next morning when she walked into the kitchen and saw the stunningly voluptuous woman seated at the table across from Hunter, sipping a cup of coffee and looking as if she belonged there.

Her tousled hair and the fact that all she seemed to be wearing was one of Hunter's flannel shirts—which came nearly to the knees of her very shapely legs—suggested she'd not just arrived.

The pain was sharp and instantaneous, going directly to Gillian's heart.

"Good morning," she said in as calm a voice as she could muster.

''Hello.'' The woman smiled up at her, her eyes as dark as Bambi's but a great deal sexier. They were also filled with the same sympathy Gillian had witnessed in Dylan's gaze. ''You must be Gillian. I'm Toni Maggione.... A—'' she paused just a heartbeat, but long enough for Gillian to understand that she was choosing her words carefully ''—colleague of Hunter's at the brain factory.''

''How nice for you.''

Knowing that Hunter had set this scene up, and understanding why, Gillian decided the situation didn't require her best manners. She turned toward him.

''You really are an idiot.''

He'd donned that damn inscrutable mask she'd come to detest. When he arched a dark brow in that silent, mocking way she recalled all too well from her first days at his house, Gillian resisted, just barely, picking up the coffee carafe and throwing it at his head.

''If you wanted me to leave, you didn't have to stage this ridiculous soap opera scene. You could have just asked. After all,'' she reminded him, ''the deal was I'd do whatever you wanted.''

Unlike last night, when he'd obviously been too uncomfortable to look at her, Hunter met her hurt, angry gaze straight on. His eyes were like two dark stones. ''And I trust you to live up to it. Which is why you'll let Ben take you back to the mainland this morning.''

Gillian glanced out the window and saw Ben Adams's truck parked outside the kitchen door. He was sitting in the driver's seat, motor running, exhaust turning the air blue.

She decided to give him one last chance to come to his senses. "That's truly what you want?"

His granite jaw was set, his expression unyielding. "Yes."

"An idiot," she repeated. Then left the kitchen.

"She's right, you know," Toni said as she lifted her cup to her full red lips. "I'm always willing to help out a friend, even if it does mean dragging my poor jet-lagged body out of a nice warm bed at dawn to drive over here. But this staged soap opera scenario, which I warned you wouldn't fool any intelligent woman for a moment, has to be the most idiotic idea you've ever come up with, darling."

"I know." Hunter dragged his good hand down his face. But he did not, could not, go after Gillian.

HUNTER WAS QUIETLY GOING insane. Despite Toni's assertion that Gillian hadn't believed they'd slept together, the ploy had worked, just as he'd hoped it would.

Gillian was gone. Just as he'd wanted.

She was safe. Just as he'd planned.

Two weeks to the day after he'd let Gillian walk out of his house, he got a telephone call from the general, informing him that the FBI, working with the CIA, had identified his attacker as a member of a radical splinter group working out of New York with ties to the Balkans.

They'd picked up the other members, all were in

federal custody, so Hunter was free to continue his work without concern about any further attacks.

And by the way, how close was he to being finished?

"It'll be done when it's done," Hunter said. He hung up on the general, hit redial, and called Ben Adams.

Hunter hadn't been surprised when he'd discovered that Gillian had immediately gone looking for work. A little investigation had discovered that she'd signed to replace a performer who'd eaten some bad shrimp and come down with food poisoning during a New England holiday concert tour.

He'd employed a similar antidote to life for years. It was, after all, difficult to think about your personal problems, your desires, or even those secret wishes of the heart, dreams you wouldn't—or couldn't— even admit to yourself, when you were buried in work.

The problem this time was, he also hadn't been able to get any work done when all he could think about was the woman he'd stupidly let slip out of his fingers. Still uneasy with the idea of love, of being loved, he tried to tell himself that what he missed was the sex.

"You're not only an idiot," he muttered as he gave up and threw a change of clothing into a duffel bag. "You're a damn liar. It's Gillian you really miss."

Despite suspecting that she would have resisted leaving the island, even if he had told her the truth— that he was only trying to protect her—Hunter knew that he'd handled things badly.

This time it would be different, he vowed. He didn't exactly have a plan. But he was an intelligent man. He'd think of something.

"It's about time you went after the girl," Ben Adams declared as he piloted the mail boat through the choppy winter waves to the mainland. "You gonna bring her back with you?"

"I don't know."

Hunter wasn't sure what he'd do if Gillian refused to see him. To talk with him. Despite having been away from civilization for a number of years, he suspected that the law would frown on him kidnapping her, tying her up and dragging her back to Castle Mountain with him, where she belonged.

"Not that I'd be one to be tellin' you what to do," Ben drawled. "But if you could manage to get her back here by tomorrow, I'd be grateful."

Hunter dragged his gaze from the steely waves. "What's happening tomorrow?"

"It's Christmas," Ben reminded him. "It's also the day I've got in the poll."

"Poll?" Hunter stared at him. "Are you saying there's actually a poll going about my personal life?"

"Ayuh," the older man agreed. "The missus wanted today, but Dr. Prescott already had that one blocked out, so she ended up with December twenty-sixth." He frowned. "She t'weren't too happy about that."

Hunter tried to recall a time when he'd seen Mildred Adams happy about anything and drew a blank. "Dylan's in it, too?"

"'Bout everyone on the island joined in. Costs five

bucks to enter. I've got my eye on a new motor for my fishing boat," he volunteered. "In case you'd be thinking about Christmas," he repeated.

"I'll keep that in mind," Hunter said dryly.

"You know," Deke said as he sprawled his lanky body in a chair in Gillian's postage-stamp-size dressing room and watched the makeup artist transform her into the larger-than-life star the audience was expecting, "this is supposed to be the season of good will."

"So they tell me." The eyeliner, which wouldn't look nearly so heavy beneath the bright stage lights, made her eyes look even larger than usual. But haunted. She frowned, thinking that she reminded herself of those paintings of wide-eyed waifs that had once been all the rage. Which wasn't at all the image she wanted to portray on the concert stage.

"Then perhaps you'd better perk up a bit before you go out there. You look like you're in the mood to play funeral dirges."

Echoing his observation, the makeup woman grumbled about Gillian's red-rimmed eyes, and did her best to cover the pink puffiness with a white crayon.

"I'll be fine," Gillian lied. In truth, she'd been far from fine since leaving Castle Mountain. She hadn't wanted to miss Hunter. But she did. Horribly. Constantly.

"I wouldn't expect your performance to be anything but spectacular. But it's not your public persona I'm concerned about. We're friends, Gilly. If you've got a problem—and it's obvious that you do—I want to help."

"It's undoubtedly a man," the makeup woman, who'd been with Gillian nearly as long as Deke, offered as she handed Gillian a tissue to blot her lips, which instead of the usual virginal pastel pink were tonight a glossy crimson.

"What makes you so sure of that?" Deke asked her.

The sixty-something woman shrugged as she added some much-needed blusher to Gillian's too pale cheeks. "Isn't it always?"

Not wanting to even attempt to explain her complex relationship with Hunter, even to her best friend, Gillian was relieved when the five-minute knock sounded on the closed door, causing the others to leave the room so she could slip out of the robe and into tonight's performance gown.

ONCE HE REACHED the mainland, Hunter rented a car and drove to Boston, where Gillian was performing, and managed to talk a tuxedo-clad man standing in line to get into the theater into selling him one of the sold-out tickets for an outrageously inflated price.

His seat was in a balcony draped with fir boughs for the season, not as near to the stage as he would have liked, but close enough that he could feel the emotions pouring from her fingertips as she played the music of her heart. The music she'd written while living with him. The music that echoed the passion of their time together. The heights of pleasure along with the depths of despair. For the first time, listening to the melancholy he knew that he was responsible for, Hunter was forced to wonder if, even as open-hearted as she was, Gillian would be able to find it in her heart to forgive him.

Strangely, when the mood of the piece changed, and she began pounding out her pent-up anger in base chords that vibrated through him, he felt a bit more reassured. After all, he tried to tell himself, an angry woman was not an indifferent one.

She looked incredible, as she always did, whether in formal wear, jeans or the seductive lingerie he'd so enjoyed buying for her. She was wearing a floor-length velvet dress. He supposed it was a concession to Christmas that she'd chosen a deep-forest-green trimmed in gold braid at the sleeves and hem rather than her usual black. She'd also changed her hair. Instead of flowing free the way he preferred it, the way she'd worn it at Stonehenge, it had been fashioned into some sort of complicated braided twist that made her look far more sophisticated and remote than the high-spirited, uninhibited woman who, in what often felt like a distant dream time, had ridden him like a wild woman. Or laughed and loved with him at Winterfest.

Indeed, if it wasn't for the slight change in her music, an even deeper emotional quality and sensuality she'd acquired while on the island, he might have thought he'd imagined their entire time together.

The audience gave her a standing ovation. Then demanded three encores. They obviously loved her. As did he.

15

AFTERWARD, WHEN IT BECAME apparent that she wasn't going to come back onto the stage, Hunter walked out into the lobby and located an usher.

"I was wondering if you could help me," he asked.

The woman smiled up at him. Her gaze slid momentarily to his cheek, but she didn't flinch as the ticket taker had, which made him think that he might stand a chance.

"With what, sir?"

"I'd like to get backstage."

Her glossy rosy lips turned down in a frown. "I'm sorry, but that's impossible."

If she'd been a male, Hunter would have tried a bribe. Since she was a lissome young blonde in her mid-twenties, he opted for a different tack.

"I understand. I suppose it serves me right. After what I did." He sighed and half turned away.

She bit at the verbal bait, as he'd hoped she would. "What did you do?"

"Ms. Cassidy and I were..." He paused, as if seeking an appropriate word. "Well...close." He dragged his good hand through his hair. "Actually, the truth is that we were in love with each other."

"I see." Her eyes narrowed.

"But I waited too long to tell her. So she finally got tired of waiting to hear the words and left me."

He decided details of Gillian's departure and the pitiful ruse he'd try to pull with Toni would only muddy the conversational waters.

"That was two long weeks ago. I've been going crazy ever since."

Hunter watched her mull that little piece of information over. Watched her eyes slide over to a doorway across the lobby. When she gave a faint, almost regretful shake of her head that hinted she was not as easily swayed as he'd hoped, the little piece of holly she was wearing pinned to a clip in her long hair gave him a bit of inspiration.

"It's difficult to be alone anytime. But I'd guess that I'm not the only person in the world who finds it especially hard at Christmas."

"Yes." A distant memory seemed to cloud her bright blue eyes for a moment. "It can be a difficult time to be alone." She pondered that some more as she chewed thoughtfully on the tip of a French-manicured thumbnail.

Hunter summoned up his best smile. The same one he used to drag out back in the days when he was forced to attend all those cocktail parties and stifling, boring teas, doing his best to charm much needed research dollars out of checkbooks in a way that had always reminded him uncomfortably of shaking leaves off money trees.

"I'm honestly not some crazed stalker, if that's what you're thinking."

A faint color darkened her cheekbones, but she

didn't assure him that the idea hadn't occurred to her. "Perhaps there is something I can do," she mused.

He widened the smile until his jaw ached. "Any help you could give me would be greatly appreciated."

"I can have Bernard go backstage with you."

"That sounds great to me." Hunter had no idea who Bernard was, but was willing to do whatever it took to get to Gillian. "Thank you."

He thought about assuring her that if he succeeded in winning Gillian over, they'd name their firstborn after her, but decided that might be overkill. He also remembered all too well about Gillian's accusation that he could be a bit Stone Age in his approach to romance and decided that she'd undoubtedly prefer to be included in such a personal decision.

Bernard turned out to be the usher's boyfriend, who'd dropped by the theater to take her out for a bite to eat after work. He was also a Boston cop.

"If Ms. Cassidy doesn't want to see you, you're out of here," he told Hunter as they walked back through the winding hallways lined with theater props from other performances.

"Absolutely," Hunter agreed. He may be an idiot, but even he wouldn't argue with an armed guy who could have doubled for the Incredible Hulk.

The dressing room door was open. The small room, not as large as his master bathroom, was filled to overflowing with people. Designer perfumes mingled with the crisp scent of the tabletop Christmas tree he saw in the corner adorned with small white lights that reminded him of attending Winterfest with Gillian.

Which wasn't that unusual, since everything reminded him of her.

The long velvet gown left her porcelain shoulders bare and made her hair gleam like fire. Diamonds flashed at her ears and on her wrist. Smudges of artfully applied makeup made her eyes appear even larger than usual in her exquisite face, and her lips, smiling up at a tall, handsome man who was wearing a trendy black silk shirt with his tuxedo, were not the soft seashell color they'd been on her video, but the scarlet of the siren he knew that she was, deep inside that sophisticated, polished European-schooled exterior.

She was the most stunningly beautiful woman he'd ever seen. Inside and out. Unfortunately, as he watched her accept the gilt-rimmed flute of champagne from a guy who could have walked off the cover of *GQ*, and of whom she seemed more than a little fond, Hunter reluctantly realized that she was also the most unapproachable.

Timing, Hunter thought grimly, was everything. She could have been Queen of the Realm, holding court, accepting the gifts and praises of her people who lived in this rarefied kingdom of arts, privilege and wealth. During their weeks together, Hunter had not only watched how seriously she took her career, and how hard she worked at her music, but he'd begun to remember the girl she'd once been. A too-thin, too-serious child who, whenever he visited the Cassidy house, was playing away on her precious piano.

She'd obviously spent years working toward this

pinnacle of success; she deserved such glowing moments in the limelight.

Even a man with his less-than-stellar social skills could figure out that this was not the time to even attempt to discuss their unconventional relationship.

He turned toward Bernard. "Would you do me a favor?"

"Depends on what it is," the man answered with typical cop suspicion.

"Would you give Ms. Cassidy a note for me?"

Bernard looked from Hunter to Gillian, who was laughing merrily at something the man who'd handed her the champagne had said.

"Make it quick," he muttered, his formerly stony expression revealing a reluctant sympathy that Hunter hated.

He scrawled a brief note on the back of his program, handed it over to the usher's hulk of a boyfriend, then, although it wasn't his first choice, left the theater.

Deciding that he didn't want to wait until morning to drive up to Maine and catch Ben's mail boat, he headed to the airport, where he managed to charter a plane and pilot for ten times the going rate because it was, after all, the pilot reminded him, Christmas Eve.

A little more than ten hours after he'd set out to bring Gillian home, Hunter was back in his library, staring out at the midnight sky. Waiting.

"THAT WAS A GREAT SHOW TONIGHT."

"Thank you." Gillian was alone with Deke, but

she wasn't sitting at her dressing table, taking off her stage makeup. Instead, she was pacing the floor of the minuscule dressing room, Hunter's note crumpled in her fist. "I thought it went well," she murmured absently. "Everyone seemed to like the new pieces."

"They were dynamite. The best you've ever done. But I wasn't talking about the show on the stage. I was talking about the show after the concert. The one you pulled off in here before your admiring fans."

"Oh?" She stopped when she reached the closed door and shot him a look over her bare shoulder. "What show would that be?"

"You know very well that you might have been smiling at all the right times, and saying all the right things, but your mind was somewhere else. Especially after the Incredible Hunk gave you that note."

She opened her curled fingers enough to read it one more time, still unable to believe that even Hunter could be so obtuse.

"Have you ever been in love?"

"Sure. About once a month. There was that brunette in Rio, and the redhead in Dublin, and that blond surfer in Sydney—"

"I'm not talking about infatuation," she said, continuing to pace in the opposite direction. "Or even lust." Though she'd become well acquainted with that feeling in the past month. "I'm talking about love. Real, forever and ever, amen type of love."

"Ah." He nodded. "That explains the change in the music. So, what's the problem? Is the guy too stupid to realize what a gem you are?"

"Actually he's the most brilliant man I've ever met. And perhaps the most stupid," she decided.

"Most men are, when it comes to love. And not to take his side in whatever fight you've obviously had, but most guys are also scared to death by the idea."

"Hunter isn't afraid of anything." She'd reached the wall and turned around yet again.

"Wanna bet?"

"What I want is to have his children."

"Well." Deke let out a long breath. "That's straight and to the point. I guess this is where I mention that you're not going to get pregnant pacing the floor here with me."

"You're right." Gillian stopped pacing and made her decision. "Do you think you can find me a flight to Castle Mountain, Maine?"

"You know I'd do anything for you, Gilly. But this is Christmas Eve. And I've never heard of Castle Mountain."

"It's an island."

"Does it even have an airstrip?"

"A small one." She'd seen it when Hunter had taken her to Winterfest. It was located on the far side of the village. It also lacked any tower or terminal, which is why most people seemed to find it easier to take Ben Adams's mail boat from the mainland, which could accommodate jets.

"I'll see what I can do."

"Thank you." She went up on her toes and kissed his cheek. "You're a true friend."

"Just make sure I get an invitation to the wedding."

"Are you kidding? I couldn't get married without you." Despite her continued pique at Hunter, Gillian smiled. "Who'd take care of all the details?"

She might never get jet lag, but that didn't mean that she enjoyed flying. She particularly didn't enjoy being in a small propeller-driven plane flying through the inky night sky over water.

The sensible thing, she'd told herself over and over again, would have been to simply land on the mainland, wait until daylight, then have Ben Adams ferry her across to Castle Mountain. But she hadn't been sure his mail boat would be operating on Christmas Day. There was also the little fact that she'd never been the least bit sensible where Hunter was concerned.

She could have made him wait. Possibly, she should have made him wait. But she was so furious, she feared she'd implode from pent-up feelings if she didn't just face him down once and for all.

The note the enormous Boston city policeman had passed on to her really was outrageous, even for Hunter.

"Gillian," he had scrawled in that bold, firm script she recalled all too well from the first note, "as you once pointed out, our deal was for thirty days. You still owe me seven of those days. If you do not live up to your end of the bargain, I will have no choice but to go public about your father. As always, the choice is yours."

"Idiot," she muttered as she glared out into the darkness.

"Did you say something?" the pilot, sitting beside her, asked.

That was another thing Hunter was going to pay for, Gillian decided. After issuing his terse summons, he could damn well pick up the tab of this charter flight. She'd considered herself fortunate when the pilot had been landing from a previous flight when she and Deke had arrived up at the airport. That was before she'd heard how much he was charging her to fly to Castle Mountain.

"It's Christmas Eve," he'd reminded her when she'd complained about the horrendously inflated rate.

"I was just talking to myself," she said now.

"Seems to be a lot of that tonight."

Engrossed in planning all the things she was going to say to Hunter, enjoying the idea of him on his knees, apologizing for all his outrageous behavior of late, Gillian didn't give any thought to the pilot's murmured comment. Nor did she respond.

But she did smile slightly at the mental image of Hunter forced to feed her breakfast in bed every morning until their tenth anniversary.

HE'D WANTED HER TO COME. But when Hunter opened the kitchen door and discovered that Gillian was the one pounding on it, Hunter's heart sank.

"What the hell are you doing here?" He purposefully made his tone cold and decidedly unwelcoming, in the hopes he could drive her away again.

"Don't play the absentminded genius with me,

Hunter.'' She threw the wadded-up concert program at his chest. ''You summoned me, remember?''

''How did you get here so soon?'' She was still clad in the green velvet gown she'd performed in, covered by a hooded black cape. Hunter glanced over her shoulder, wondering if she was alone.

''I chartered a plane in Boston, then rented a jeep from the very nice man whom the pilot dragged out of his house for the second time tonight to plow the runway. He says, by the way, that he hopes we're both going to stay put because he's still got a dollhouse and a miniature racing track to finish putting together before his kids get up in the morning....

''It's also a very good thing you're rich, because I probably could have flown first class to Paris for what it's going to cost you to bring me here on Christmas Eve.''

''Christmas Day,'' he corrected her. Midnight had come and gone, which, Hunter thought irrelevantly, meant that Ben had won the poll.

''I hate it when you get nitpicky,'' she muttered. ''Speaking of which, you're getting careless, Hunter.'' Because he was still surprised by her arrival, she managed to slip past him into the kitchen. ''All the security gates were open.''

She tossed her beaded evening bag onto the kitchen table, then turned and sucked in a harsh breath as she realized Hunter was not alone. A blond man in an open, obviously custom-tailored cashmere coat over a thick ski sweater was standing behind him, holding a very ugly steel pistol at the back of Hunter's dark head.

"Who are you?"

Hunter cursed beneath his breath. "He's James Van Horn," he said. "From the State Department. He's also the guy in charge of my most recent assassination attempt."

She paled just a little, but a lot less than most people would have under the circumstances, Hunter thought, and her eyes filled with speculation rather than terror.

"Why would you want to kill Hunter after paying him so much money for his project?"

She'd no sooner asked the question when Hunter watched the comprehension dawn in those intelligent green eyes. "You're not after its peacekeeping possibilities, are you?"

"That theory's unproved."

The man growled the first words he'd spoken since instructing Hunter to send her away before opening the door. His tone confirmed that Gillian had hit close to the truth.

"Surely the State Department isn't in on this?"

"Van Horn's turned free agent," Hunter said. "Seems he's been holding bidding wars for my program. Now that he's settled on a buyer, all he needs is the merchandise."

"You'll never get it," Gillian told the man on a flare of heat.

As she tried to remain calm, she studied the man. He appeared too suave and handsome to be a traitor, but then again, she realized that the only traitors she'd ever actually seen were in the movies.

"Your lover was proving annoyingly uncooperative." Van Horn told Gillian nothing she couldn't have guessed for herself. "But I do believe that fate may have just provided the necessary impetus."

"Touch a hair on her head, Van Horn, and I'll kill you with my bare hands." Hunter's face was grim, his eyes ice. "Let her leave now, and I'll give you the damn program code."

"Hunter!" Gillian was staring at him. "You can't let this...this...bully take over the world."

"I'll do whatever it takes to make you safe," he told her. "The program isn't any good without the codes," he reminded Van Horn. "Let her go and you've got it all. Hell, I'll even give you a tutorial on how to use the data."

"Hunter," Gillian repeated, "you can't possibly be serious! I'm not going to let you turn traitor on my account."

"Is she always this stubborn?" Van Horn asked with a flare of frustration as he moved closer to her.

"Pretty much," Hunter said.

The man's curse was coarse and vicious. "We'll just have to teach her to stay the hell out of places—and things—where she doesn't belong." He twisted Gillian's arm with a harsh brute force that made her cry out.

The pained sound earned the ire of the forgotten cat, who'd been watching the exchange from her box beside the stove.

With an earsplitting howl, she launched herself at the man who was harming the woman who'd fed her bacon and saved her kittens from the sea. Claws tangled in his blond hair, raked down his face, dug into his chest.

Hunter used the welcome distraction to grab for Gillian, who'd been thrown off balance as Van Horn fought off the furious, determined animal clinging to his sweater.

Before he could get her to the door, the sound of a shot shattered the silence of the night.

Hunter watched, horrified, as a red stain blossomed like a deadly poppy on the front of her cape. Then spread.

"Hunter?" Gillian's eyes were glazed with shock; her face had turned the unhealthy color of rice paper.

"It's okay, baby." He had a choice. To pull her to him and never let go, or to try to prevent Van Horn from killing them both. "Just hold on. Everything's going to be fine."

With that promise, and a red haze of fury obscuring his gaze, he threw himself at her attacker, who'd finally managed to shake off the cat.

The force caused Van Horn to drop the pistol, but before Hunter could make a dive for it, Van Horn grabbed the cleaver from Mrs. Adams's knife rack and swung it with both hands like an ancient Scots Highlander wielding a claymore.

Hunter raised his left arm to block the attack aimed at his chest, then cursed as the blade sliced through his shirt into flesh. Grinding his teeth against the pain, he lowered his head and charged, slamming into Van Horn's chest and knocking him off balance.

As the two men rolled across the floor, slugging and kicking, Hunter discovered he was at a distinct disadvantage when his injured arm would not—or could not—obey the commands of his brain.

Van Horn slammed a fist into Hunter's face; in turn, Hunter drove his knee upward, into the other man's groin. With a bellow of rage, Van Horn rolled off him and staggered to his knees, chest heaving.

He raised the vicious cleaver over his head; the blade glistened in the bright overhead light. Blood dripped from its razor sharp edge.

With his left arm useless, Hunter was struggling to get to his feet when another shot exploded.

Van Horn's eyes widened in obvious shock. Then rolled back into his head. Deflating like a leaking balloon, he was dead when he hit the floor.

Hunter managed to crawl to Gillian. "Sweetheart, give me the gun." He had to pry it from her rigid fingers. "It's all right."

"He was going to kill you." Her eyes were glazed, her frail voice little more than a whisper.

"Thanks to you, he's not going to be able to hurt anyone ever again." Not wanting any accidents to make a bad situation worse, he put the still loaded gun out of reach.

"Am I going to die?"

"Of course not. You're going to be just fine." He ripped open her long wool cape, discovered the wound that was spurting bright red blood onto the bodice of the green velvet dress and prayed that it would be true.

Her legs had turned to rubber, her body to ice. She was shivering like a woman caught up in the grips of a deadly fever. He clutched her to him as he tried to reach the receiver of the wall phone with his good hand, but she was too weak to help and the distance was too great.

"I'm just going to lie you down for a second," he said. "So I can call 911 and get us some help." Hating to let go of her for even a moment, Hunter had no choice but to lower her carefully, gently, to the pine plank floor.

The cat immediately curled up beside her, pressing its orange and black fur against her side.

"Hunter?"

He could barely hear her whisper his name over the chattering of her teeth and the hammering of his heart.

"I'm here, sweetheart." He punched in the speed dial. "I won't leave you."

Her eyes were unfocused, but her lips curved in what he allowed himself to believe was a faint smile. "I love you."

Her lids fluttered closed. The emergency dispatcher answered on the first ring. As he felt Gillian drifting further and further away from him, Hunter only hoped it was soon enough.

He held her against his chest, his lips buried in her lush, fiery cloud of hair. As he waited for the paramedics to arrive, Hunter made deal after deal with the God that he'd almost managed to convince himself he'd stopped believing in.

16

GILLIAN DREAMED she was stumbling though a blizzard. She was cold, so cold. Deadly cold. She was surrounded by a blinding white world, disoriented, lost. Somewhere in the far distance she heard Hunter calling her name, over and over again, but she couldn't see him. Couldn't find him.

She stumbled into a deep drift and tried to call back to him, to let him know where she was, so he could rescue her. But her lips had turned to stone, and her mind, fogged in icy white clouds, could not think of the words.

"I love you." The words came from her heart rather than her head, and as she felt the snow caving in on her, like an avalanche, she wasn't sure whether she'd managed to say them out loud.

Hunter was still calling to her. He sounded closer, but with his voice muffled by the gale-force winds that had begun to blow, she couldn't be certain.

She tried to reach for him, but her strength had strangely deserted her and her hand was too heavy.

She grew colder. And tired. So, so tired.

She whispered his name, like a prayer. Then closed her eyes and surrendered to the swirling whiteness.

IT WAS BRIGHT. TOO BRIGHT. Gillian closed her eyes against the blinding light.

"Gillian." The voice was deep and wonderfully familiar. "Open your eyes. It's all over, sweetheart. You're going to be all right."

She struggled to do as he asked, looking up at him through slitted eyes. "Hunter?"

"It's me, baby. You're going to be just fine," he reassured her again.

"I'm not dead?"

"Of course you're not." Even as groggy as she was, Gillian could recognize the false heartiness in his tone. Along with relief.

She blinked and tried to focus. "Then why are you wearing a halo?"

She'd drifted back into the soft fog before hearing his answer.

ONCE SHE'D BEEN WHEELED into the recovery room after surgery, Hunter refused to leave Gillian's side. For three excruciatingly long days he sat hunched in the plastic chair, seeking the faintest sign of awareness, talking reassuringly to her during those brief periods when she'd opened her eyes, monitoring her breathing and watching the reassuring peaks of the green line moving across the monitor over the hospital bed while she slept.

Dylan arrived to hold vigil with him, as did Bram and Toni, although Toni refrained from going into the ICU for fear that Gillian might awaken and be unduly upset by her presence. Julianna and Charity took turns, one visiting the hospital while the other minded their children.

Even Mildred and Ben Adams dropped by each morning and evening. Since he refused to leave Gillian to go to the cafeteria, Mildred brought him hot meals which, in her own formidable way, she'd insist he eat.

On the fourth morning, Hunter had dozed off when a soft voice he'd so desperately feared he would never hear again roused him from the turmoiled sleep filled with vivid reenactments of that horrifying incident in his kitchen he knew he'd never forget.

"You're awake." Relief and joy sounded in his head like the entire Mormon Tabernacle Choir singing hosannas to the heavens.

"I think I am." Gillian blinked, but this time her eyes were clearer than they'd been for days. "I know this is a cliché, but where am I?"

"On Castle Mountain. In the hospital."

"I dreamed you were an angel."

"It was the overhead light. I was leaning over you, blocking part of it out. The doctor said that happens a lot when people first come out of the anesthetic."

"Oh." Her smooth brow furrowed. "The last thing I remember is being in a plane. Did it crash?"

"No. You were shot." Hunter would never stop feeling guilty about that.

"Shot?" She frowned, obviously trying to remember. "Not in the plane, surely?"

"In the kitchen. Four days ago."

"Four days?" Her eyes widened. Surprise had them clearing a bit more.

He nodded. "And I've been going crazy every one of them."

"I vaguely remember being in the kitchen." Her frown of concentration deepened. "There was a man there...."

"Van Horn."

"The man from the State Department. He was going to shoot you. Then he grabbed me." She rubbed her temple. "I can't recall what happened next."

"Your crazy cat saved you."

"She attacked him." Her lips quirked slightly at the corners. "Like a tigress. That's the last thing I remember. Everything else between then and when you became an angel is a blank."

It was just as well, Hunter decided. The lifesaving measures he'd witnessed in the emergency room were not the stuff of pretty memories.

She rubbed the front of the peppermint-pink hospital gown. "My chest hurts."

"You've got a cracked rib, among other things. And they had to put in a chest tube because the bullet ended up in your lung." It had been horrific at the time, yet not as bad, the emergency room doctor had assured him, as it would have been if it had hit her heart.

"The idea of a bullet anywhere in my body boggles the mind," she murmured. She touched her temple, as if it was giving her a headache.

"Van Horn's gun went off and you were in the way. I suppose I'll never know if he was aiming at me, or if it was a wild shot caused by him trying to pull the cat loose.

"I do know that the whole thing was my fault. If

I hadn't forced you to come back to me, you never would have stumbled into his attempt to steal my research.''

"You left me a note," she recalled. "At the theater.'' The frown deepened. Annoyance darkened her eyes. Grateful for any show of emotion, Hunter welcomed it. He also knew he deserved it. "Demanding I fulfill my agreement.''

"It was a stupid idea,'' he admitted. He raked his hand through his hair. "I thought about begging, but figured you might want to stay away for a longer time, just to make me suffer for a while.

"Which you would have been entitled to do,'' he added quickly. "But then, when I began to write the note, it crossed my mind that if I made you angry enough, you'd come home right away.''

She stared at him. "For a supposedly brilliant man,'' she said slowly, "that was, without a doubt, your most idiotic idea yet.''

"I know.''

He watched as she licked her lips, then he belatedly poured some water from the carafe beside the bed into a glass, lifted her into a sitting position and held the plastic glass to her lips.

She sipped thirstily, as if fluid hadn't been forced through her wounded body for days through the needle in the back of her hand, then sank back onto the pillow.

"Well, idiotic or not, your ploy obviously worked. Because here I am. They didn't get it, did they?''

"Get what?''

"Your program. Van Horn didn't have evil cohorts backing him up?''

"No. He was a maverick. The only partner he had was the guy I threw over the cliff, and he turned out to be a former Special Forces guy turned mercenary for hire. But it didn't matter that Van Horn was alone. Because I was prepared to give him everything he wanted the minute you walked in the door."

She gave him one of her long, solemn looks, the kind that made him think she was looking all the way to his soul. "You really meant that." It was not a question.

"Absolutely."

"Even though you've spent years working on it, even though it nearly got you killed on three separate occasions that we know of, you would have given all your research to that horrid man?"

"In a heartbeat. I would have given him anything he wanted to save you. Because without you, Gillian, I don't have a damn thing."

"It's about time you realized that..." A sudden recollection flashed across her face. "Van Horn hurt your arm." She touched her fingers to his sleeve, which effectively covered up the bandage the ER doctor had applied.

"It's just a scratch." He brushed some tangled curls back from her forehead. "Thanks to you."

"He's dead, isn't he?"

"Yeah. Are you okay with that?"

Gillian's brow furrowed. "Yes." Her eyes cleared. "I think I am."

"Good... You should rest. We can talk about all this later."

"That scene with the woman in your kitchen, your

colleague from the brain factory, was another foolish act of desperation, too, wasn't it?''

''Absolutely, and Toni warned me that it was unnecessarily harsh, but I was desperate to get you away from the island in case someone might try to hurt you to get to me.'' Which was exactly what had happened. Thanks to his idiocy.

''I suppose that makes some cockeyed sense. Though I should have been allowed to make my own decision about whether or not to leave. But if you were afraid I'd be harmed, why did you insist I come back?''

''Because I'd been assured that all the terrorists had been rounded up. But mostly because I missed you like hell.''

''Good.'' She nodded. ''So you really didn't sleep with her that night after we came home from Winterfest?''

''Of course not. I haven't wanted any woman since I saw your video. I'll never want any other woman, as long as I live.''

''I didn't think you had.'' She smiled and Hunter felt as if the sun had finally come out from behind a lifetime of clouds. ''You know, Hunter, you still haven't told me.''

''Told you what?''

''That you love me.''

''Is there any question?''

''No.'' She lifted the hand that didn't have the needle in it to his cheek. ''But it would be nice to hear the words.''

He took a deep breath, laced their fingers together and brought their joined hands to his lips. ''I love you." He touched his mouth to her wrist. Then to the purplish-blue bruise at the inside curve of her elbow. "You have to believe me, Gillian, I've never said that to any other woman before."

She managed a soft laugh at that declaration. "Oh, I definitely believe you, Hunter."

"I think I started falling in love with you from the beginning, maybe even when I saw the tape. But it was too new. Too scary, and I didn't know how to handle it. So I tried to convince myself it was only lust."

"Lust isn't all bad."

"No." He managed his first smile in days. "But lust with love is a helluva lot better." He worked his way up her arm, pushing aside the gown to brush a string of kisses along her collarbone. "And I really do love you." The second time was easier, Hunter discovered. He was actually beginning to enjoy saying the words. "I love you."

He nuzzled her neck, drank in her unique scent that all the antiseptic hospital smells in the world couldn't quite cover up. "I'll always love you."

"It's about time you smartened up." Her voice was still not as strong as normal, but Hunter could hear the humor in it. Humor he realized had allowed her to survive a bleak and affectionless childhood. A humor that had helped her put up with him.

"There's more," he said.

Because he was all too tempted to join her in that narrow bed, and because he knew that she was a long way from being ready to be tumbled, he gave her a satisfying kiss on the lips, then sat back down in the chair. But he did not release her hand.

"Oh?"

"I want to make an honest woman of you."

"How chivalrous," she said dryly. "But as it turned out, that was one bullet we dodged, Hunter. I'm not pregnant."

"I was sort of hoping to change that. As soon as possible after we spring you from this joint."

She glanced around the stark room, then up at the IV bags hanging beside the bed. "The sooner the better," she decided. "We were both only children, and while that's fine for some people, I'll want a big family."

"You've got it. Name the number. Six, nine, twelve, hell, we'll have a baker's dozen, if you'd like." He could keep adding rooms on to the house until doomsday, Hunter decided.

"I like your enthusiasm, Hunter." It was her turn to lift their hands to her lips. Above them her eyes, which had glazed with near-death only days ago, sparkled with the saucy spirit he'd come to love. "But somewhere between four and an even half dozen should suffice. Since I'm the one who'll be actually doing all the work...

"I've also been thinking about the cameras," she murmured.

"Cameras?"

"The ones you have stashed all over the house," she said with amazing aplomb for a woman who'd been spied on.

"You knew?"

"Of course. After you mentioned being able to hear me play back in your office, I went looking for them while you were away at the brain factory. And although part of me finds the idea appealingly kinky, an even stronger part insists on some privacy. I've decided they can stay. So long as we agree ahead of time when they're turned on.''

"Absolutely.'' Hunter hadn't been aware of holding his breath until he let it out on a huge whoosh. "It's a deal.''

"And the kittens stay, as well.''

"I wouldn't take them away from their mother.'' After having watched the cat's ferocity, he wouldn't dare try.

"I also want a dog. I never had a dog and I think one would be good for the children.''

"It's yours. Whatever you want, Gillian, children, dogs, emeralds, the moon, the stars, you name it, and I'll move heaven and earth to get it for you.''

She smiled. Then gingerly lifted the hand that was attached to the IV and crooked her finger, coaxing him closer.

"Emeralds are nice. Children are even better. But you needn't go to all that trouble, Hunter.'' She splayed her fingers on the back of his head and drew his lips to hers. "Because if I had to narrow the entire world down to one thing, all I'd really want is you.''

"I'm yours.'' Because he was still worried about her, Hunter kept the kiss short. But what it lacked in length, it more than made up for in emotion. "For as long as you'll have me.''

"Why don't we begin with forever?'' Gillian suggested. "Then go from there?''

It was, they both agreed, the best idea either of them had ever had.

Epilogue

Five years later

CHAMPAGNE BUBBLED, diamonds glistened, strings from the quartet hired to play for the Broadway cast party wept, although the mood of the night was unrelentingly upbeat as the reviews continued to come in.

"'Brilliant. Haunting and emotional,'" the pretty blond actress hired to play the lead in the Gothic romantic musical read out loud. "'With a superb score that heightens the sense of moody isolation.'"

"'A must-see,'" her stage lover read from another paper. His dangerous dark looks and deep baritone voice had earned him the cover of both *People* and *Time* and had brought back the term *matinee idol.* "'The electric score is the backbone of this excellent-in-every-way musical, reminding us that show tunes can reach the loftiest of heights in the hands of a brilliantly creative composer.'"

"'Brilliant and stunning, with all the emotions of love, hate, fear, misery and love rising and falling in the score,'" the producer read from yet another review.

"*Brilliant* seems to be the word of the evening," Hunter murmured in Gillian's ear as they stood near the windows of New York City's Rainbow Room, looking down at the dazzling lights that winked like fallen stars far below.

She smiled up at him, enjoying her night of triumph. Enjoying sharing it with her husband even more. "It may be an overused word. But I have to admit that I like it."

"You are brilliant, Gillian." He put his arm around her bare shoulder and drew her to him.

The room was filled with people who had a stake in tonight's Broadway opening, along with others who just felt the need to be near success. And from the opening note of tonight's performance, it was obvious that everyone in the audience had realized that they were witnessing something special. "Which is why you deserve to have the entire world at your feet."

"It isn't exactly the entire world." But from this magical room high above the city, she could see the bright marquee with her name spelled out in lights, just as she'd always dreamed.

He chuckled. "Try telling that to your average New Yorker."

She rested her head on his shoulder and felt it happening again—Hunter's ability to shut out the world, to narrow the focus down, even in a crowd like this, to just the two of them. She'd given up trying to figure out how he did it. But there were occasions, like tonight, when she was certainly glad he possessed the somewhat eerie ability.

"Try telling any New Yorker that he's average," she countered. "I love the city," she admitted. "The vitality, the neighborhoods, the scents and sounds and food. But I'll be glad to get back home."

"I'll second that." Oblivious to any audience, he touched his lips to the top of her hair, which she'd swept up atop her head for the formal occasion. "The kids will be glad to have you back, too. When I called Mrs. Adams during intermission, she said that Sarah has composed a welcome-home song for us."

"That's sweet."

"And Spencer blew up the kitchen."

A light, airy tune had been singing in her head, but Hunter's words got her immediate attention. "He didn't!"

"Not really." He grinned. "It was just a little experiment with some baking powder that went awry. The painters should be done before we get home."

"He certainly is his father's child," Gillian said on a sigh.

"As Sarah is her mother's," Hunter pointed out. The twins had possessed remarkably individual personalities from the beginning. "Perhaps this third time we'll get a blend."

"Perhaps." Gillian smiled up at him as she touched a hand to her still-flat stomach. She'd taken the pregnancy test before getting dressed for tonight's opening performance. When she'd viewed the positive results, she'd quit worrying about any reviews. Because no matter how long she'd waited for this moment, no play was as important as this child she and Hunter had made together in love.

"Do you think I've done my duty long enough?" she asked.

The warmth in his gaze turned to alarm. "Is something wrong? Are you all right? Is it the baby?"

"Nothing's wrong, I'm fine, and the baby is, as far as I can tell at this early stage in the game, nice and cozy. I was just thinking I'd like to go back to the hotel suite and continue this celebration in private.''

His eyes darkened with a lusty speculation Gillian knew would still have the power to thrill her when she was a very old lady teaching her great-grandchildren scales on the magnificent Steinway Hunter had bought her.

''Brilliant,'' he murmured as he began leading her through the crush of partygoers.

Escape took longer than hoped, since they had to stop every few feet across the room so Gillian could accept more hugs, more air kisses aimed at her cheeks, more accolades.

''Alone at last.'' He sighed with relief as the elevator doors closed and they began the swift descent to the lobby. He leaned against the back wall and drew her into his arms. ''I thought we'd never get out of there.''

''People stay up later in New York than they do in Castle Mountain,'' she pointed out. ''Technically, the night's still young.'' She tipped her head back and lifted her face for his kiss. A slow, seductive kiss that had her toes curling in her ridiculously high Italian heels.

''I love my necklace,'' she murmured against his mouth. It was created of diamonds and emeralds set in platinum.

''I'm glad.'' The elevator came to a stop. ''Because I loved buying it for you.''

The door slid open. ''As it happens, I have a little gift for you, too,'' she murmured.

As she left the elevator in front of him, Hunter was treated to a mouthwatering display of bare flesh framed by the plunging back of the long black silk dress.

"Are you going to tell me what it is? Or do I have to wait?"

"That depends on how you feel about making mad, passionate love in a limo."

"You know me. I'm up for anything where you're concerned, sweetheart. Though getting naked in a moving vehicle has always sounded a bit tricky," he tacked on.

The limousine slid silently to the curb just as they walked out of the building. Hunter waved off the driver and opened the back door himself.

"Maybe it won't be as tricky as you think, darling." The smoldering come-hither glance Gillian shot back over her shoulder as she climbed into the long black limo was designed to bring a man to his knees.

"Oh?"

Her incredible eyes sparkled with a combination of lust and humor as bright as the precious stones she wore around her neck. "I'm not wearing any underwear."

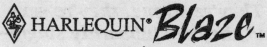

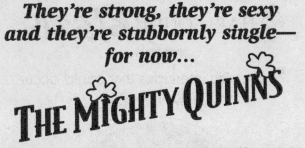

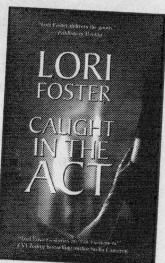